D0928912

Love your way

Fox ox ♡

The Gypsy Chronicles

The Gypsy has Three Truths:
one with me, one with you,
and one with herself.

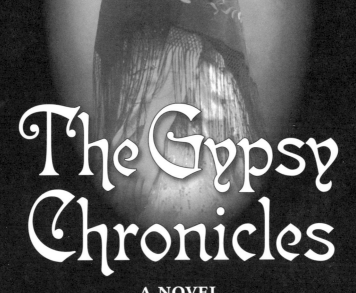

The Gypsy Chronicles

A NOVEL

ALISON MACKIE

Ashton Court Press

This book is a work of fiction.
Names, characters, places and incidents are products of the author's imagination
or are used fictitiously. Any resemblance to actual events or locales or persons,
living or dead, is entirely coincidental.

Copyright ©2006 by Alison Mackie
All rights reserved including the right to reproduce this book
or portions thereof in any form whatsoever.

Published by Ashton Court Press, Inc.
2045 Loveland Blvd., Port Charlotte, Florida, 33980 USA
JMackie@AshtonCourtPress.com.

Printed in the United States of America.

Book Design by Kathleen Edwards
The Naples Media Group

ISBN13 978-0-615-13465-9
ISBN10 0-615-13465-3

First Edition: February 2007
10 9 8 7 6 5 4 3 2 1

For information about special discounts for bulk purchases,
please contact JMackie@AshtonCourtPress.com.

Book Clubs and Reading Groups may request discussions with the author
by completing a request form at www.TheGypsyChronicles.com.

This book is for Uncle Stanley and Aunt Mary;
Love-birds extraordinaire.

The Gypsy Chronicles

A story is like water
that you heat for your bath.

It takes messages between the fire
and your skin. It lets them meet,
and it cleans you!

–Coleman Barks; Rumi

No man, as a general rule, shows his soul to another man.
He shows it only to a woman.

–Lafcadio Hearn

I didn't trust it for a moment,
but I drank it anyway,
the wine of my own poetry.

–Coleman Barks; Lal Ded

Love can sometimes be magic. But magic can sometimes …
just be an illusion.

–Javan

Introduction

*A*llow me to introduce myself: My name is Gitana, and although I am not a story teller by trade, I am the teller of this tale. Gitana is a Spanish word meaning *Gypsy woman*, and like Gypsy women everywhere, I have mastered the art of pulling information out of thin air.

Fortune telling is a simple thing really, and not nearly as mysterious as some would have you believe. How do I do it? I merely turn my sight forward and open my senses to important future events. Then, I close my eyes, reach into the shadows and pull out a story! This is where the literary term 'for-shadowing' comes from, and where story and fortune telling cross paths.

But there is time enough for the future, down the road. In order to tell this particular tale, we must begin in the past. *The Gypsy Chronicles* opens with the story of how I came to meet the great love of my life, for without him, there would be no tale to tell. Have you heard of Tzigany's Matrimonial Beds?

Upon each bed that he makes, Tzigany bestows a potent charm; one which guarantees a lifetime of loving passion within the marriage. To gaze upon one of his beds is to enliven one's soul; to sleep in one, divine! Even the King and Queen of Spain have one.

In *The Gypsy Chronicles*, we will fly from story to story; love to love; and bed to bed. However, if you were to assume this book is just about sex, you would be mistaken. There is no sex in this book, but something even finer: Love! Or should I say, quietly, the making of love... If there is something missing in your heart, you may find it returned to you, here. For, when you allow yourself to be drawn by the stronger pull of what you love, the most beautiful dream, you will discover, is your very own.

The Gypsy Chronicles is a bedtime story for grown-ups, and tonight, my friends, the subject is love!

Before we go any further, I feel obliged to inform you that the style of this tale is fashioned upon the hot air balloon, a literary genre I invented myself! Riding in a balloon generates feelings of great daring, as well as dreaminess. With no steering wheel, and only the wind to guide us, a new way of thinking is required. Massive and silent, we rise above the crowd and know that anything can happen, and does, and will.

But enough. The time has come. A current of wind hastens past and the balloon strains at the ropes, summoning us toward travel. Before this particular voyage can begin however, we must first untie the knots that fasten us to familiar territory. It promises to be an uplifting experience: The mind thus elevated offers better perspective. Are you with me?

Tzigany and Gitana

It was love at first sight! When he appeared before me, I knew with a certainty he was the man for me.

A wise woman once told me that there is no moment of charm without long roots in the past and so although we had just laid eyes upon one another, it was as though Tzigany and I had known each other our entire lives.

I had been enjoying a mid morning siesta, lying peacefully on a soft bed of wild poppies in a meadow near Seville, when his shadow passed over me.

I turned my head to see a pair of unfamiliar boots. Quality leather, hand stitched, and polished to perfection, they were very impressive to look at. Nobody in my clan was in possession of such fine boots. Who was this stranger, boldly casting his shadow upon my body?

My eyes traveled the stranger's very tall frame, straight up to his face, and when my eyes met with his, they took me in fast and deep. It was love at first sight: I would have recognized him anywhere.

"How do you do," inquired my beloved stranger, in a

pleasingly deep and mellifluous voice.

I was doing quite well, but the words were too slow in forming upon my lips, so I smiled, rolled over onto my side and raised myself upon an elbow.

The attractive stranger sat beside me on the grass and looked at me long and hard. With any other man such an intimate gaze would have insulted my honor. With any other man I would have stood up, turned on my heel and stalked off, twitching my skirt in his direction. Under Tzigany's admiring gaze however, I felt utterly content, like a cat basking in sunshine. His eyes were first drawn towards my proud well padded bottom, then to my rounded hips and last upon my melons, or bosoms as you call them.

As he studied me, I took in the full reckoning of him: Where my body was soft and round, his was hard. Like an oak. He was a man on the grand scale, larger than life. There was something exceptional in his aspect, and I knew with a certainty that I was in the presence of a very great man.

So I said to him, I said, "I have a boyfriend."

And he said, "I have a girlfriend."

And I said, "I don't care for my boyfriend, much."

And he said, "What a coincidence, I too don't care for my girlfriend…"

We bantered back and forth like that for a while. It was wonderful, just wonderful!

Then he said, "Seeing as it is fairly obvious that we are going to be married, would you allow me to kiss you?" He waggled his brow comically.

I played at being mildly shocked by his request for a kiss, but in truth I could not have been more pleased: It's alright to let a perfect stranger kiss you, so long as he is perfect. And besides, we were going to be married…

"So presumptuous!" I scolded.

"So forward!" he agreed.

I laughed. "So what are you waiting for?" My lips softened as his gaze deepened into mine.

"Do my ears deceive me, or did you just grant me permission to kiss you?" He was genuinely uncertain.

"Do my ears deceive me or did you propose marriage?" I affected a business-like attitude.

"Your ears did not deceive you, marriage is what I propose," he affirmed.

I shrugged. "Well then, seeing as we are going to be married, you may kiss me." I readied myself for the kiss by lifting my chin in his direction. He leaned towards me and kissed the top of my head. It was a mother's bedtime kiss to a child! Flashing a look of disappointment, I hooked my arm around his neck and pulled him towards my lips.

Whether it was minutes or seconds that passed, I can not say, but when our kiss was over Tzigany leaned back on his elbow.

"It would seem that I have just found for myself the perfect wife," he laughed.

"And I, the perfect husband."

We were only half joking, for the other half knew, deep in our bones, that we had already come to know the most important things about one another in our short exchange of words and kisses.

You have to understand: Before meeting Tzigany, I was always on the perimeter of everything. My sisters did not confide in me and although I was the eldest daughter, I was not my mother's favorite. My very tall stature meant that I towered above most people. Women in my clan did not warm to me and men were always, you know, a little nervous.

I did feel from time to time, a little loneliness. A faithful lover to my pillow, my arms ached to wrap around a real husband. But whom? Every suitor had one or another thing wrong with him; some little something I found impossible to overlook. I knew very well what I disliked and could spot it immediately, sometimes even before a man spoke. A stooped posture meant laziness. That would never do. I expected my future husband to be industrious. A meandering stride indicated aimlessness. Dirty fingernails, messy appearance, a laugh too loud, or a propensity to talk too much and listen too little … I could never align myself with any man flawed in these ways.

I could tell in great detail that which I did not want in a man. However, I could not say exactly what it was that I did want, only that he be someone whom I could admire. The problem with most women, I felt, is that they get all excited over nothing, and then marry him. I was determined to follow a different path.

"My name is Tzigany de Torres," he said, as if remembering something important he had forgotten to tell me.

"Your name has a very nice ring to it." I repeated it aloud, enjoying the way it rolled off my tongue. Tzigany de

Torres. His mother must have been in love with the poetry of sound.

"And I am Gitana." I replied.

"Gitana de Torres," he corrected me, and I beamed.

"This calls for a little something." He pulled two cigars from his vest pocket and placed one between my lips. Surrounded by the aromatic smoke from Havana, we celebrated our engagement between happy puffs of smoke.

I led Tzigany to my encampment. Apparently, my fiancé was notoriously famous, for when I introduced him to my parents, they recognized his name immediately and were well pleased with the aristocrat I had brought home. Apart from his impressive lineage, Tzigany was a gifted carver and carpenter, well known for his finely crafted Matrimonial Beds. He was a great artist and therefore destined for immortality.

Instinctively, my parents considered Tzigany worthy of their trust. Trust in your instinct always, they say, and you will never be wrong. Second guess your instinct and it will punish you with unreliability.

They quickly gave their consent, a dowry was negotiated and the wedding planned for the very same evening.

That night, around a blazing campfire, musicians of the clan brought out their guitars and joyful music filled the night air in celebration of our union. As the wine flowed, the revelers became increasingly animated, and so it passed unnoticed when Tzigany and I slipped away in the night, towards our future.

The Night Of Our First Excitement

Although it was dark inside of Tzigany's caravan, I could make out an immaculate space of walls lined with hundreds of books. The presence of so vast a library pleased me, for I was an avid reader myself. Of course, I would not be reading a single book for at least a year: It does not bode well for a marriage to crack the spine of a book during the honeymoon phase.

Tzigany lit a lamp and watched as I took account of my new home. I ran my fingers slowly over the spines of his books, head tilted to one side, reading the titles aloud.

"A book lover like me," he observed.

I stepped into the kitchen area and nodded with approval at the fine red enamel stove. Turning slowly, I made one last study of my surroundings before facing him.

"Tzigany, here we are on our honeymoon no less, and not a bed in sight!" I was more than a little concerned, accustomed as I was to beds folding down, berth style from caravan walls; but there, from floor to ceiling, everywhere…there were nothing but books and no sign of a bed anywhere!

Tzigany raised his brow, a gesture I had already come to recognize as his call to play. "A bed! I know there is one here somewhere." He scratched his head, as if baffled. "Now where could I have put the bed?"

"Well, you can not have misplaced it, surely. A bed is too large to misplace." I grinned, enjoying the charade.

"Truly, a bed is far too large to go missing in a space as small as this." He stretched out his arms.

"But where then?" I scratched my own head, genuinely

puzzled. Patting the book-lined walls, and knocking at the sturdy shelves, I searched high and low. Then I saw it: a latch.

"Perhaps the bed is here?" I fiddled with the latch.

"Perhaps," Tzigany said, placing his cigar between his lips. I stood back and watched as he unhooked the latch, and slid the book case open, like sliding doors. The bed that he pulled down from the wall was no ordinary bed. It unfolded lengthwise as opposed to the usual berth style. Carved beautifully within the headboard were twin doves, framed within a heart. It was the height of invention to have such a luxuriously large bed, complete with a headboard masterpiece, hidden inside so small a space as a Gypsy's caravan. I was massively impressed.

"I've married a genius!" I said.

"You think?" Again with the raised brow, and I smiled.

"I've never seen, in my entire life, such a fine bed." I turned to face him.

"Tonight will be the first time. This bed has never been slept in before. I've been waiting for the right woman, Gitana."

This unexpected sentiment touched me. Until then, he had danced around his feelings with a light playful step. We both had. Still, I could not understand why he would choose to sleep upon the floor, when so beautiful a bed was to be had.

"This is a Matrimonial Bed," he explained, "I bestowed a potent charm upon it. One does not sleep in such a bed alone."

"You *charmed* the bed?" It was my turn to raise a brow.

"What kind of charm?"

"A charm of passion that guarantees a lifetime of pleasurable lovemaking within the marriage," he related simply. "I charm all of my Matrimonial Beds. I am called a magician by some, a humanitarian by others." He laughed.

Tzigany opened the large ceiling window to the night sky. Above his head, a million stars and the moon shone brightly. I sat upon the edge of the bed and admired my new husband, whose silvery aura rivaled that of the stars. There was a whiff of the super-natural about him and I liked it. It was a grand claim to make, but if anyone could charm a bed with such potency, it was surely he. I felt a thrill coursing through my body.

"Please, tell me how you charm your beds."

Tzigany held his hands out before me, spreading his long fingers wide. He held them out in such a way that they resembled magical tools. Their muscularity dazzled me. Have you ever seen the hands of Michelangelo's David? Well, Tzigany's hands were like that; large and emanating with power. Mesmerized, I gazed upon them steadily as he spoke.

"Two hands, ten fingers, connected to one mind." He said, pointing to his skull. "Whatsoever the mind can conceive, the hands can achieve." He waggled his long fingers in the air before him like a magician. "Gitana, if you had it in your mind, you could also charm a bed. To want to is to be able to."

I shook my head. "No, I couldn't. You have a gift." In some people, one sense will dominate. For me, it is foresight. Tzigany's gift was of a rare variety that I had only read about in arcane books of knowledge.

Standing up, I turned my back and Tzigany pulled the zipper down the length of my gown. I motioned for him to lie down on the bed while I finished undressing.

He removed his boots, lay across the bed, and watched as I allowed the gown to slip off my shoulders to the floor. Piece by piece I removed my lacy underclothing until I was naked.

A confidence: Although I was virginal in body, I was hardly virginal in spirit. You have to understand that I had a secret copy of the *Kama Sutra*, the ancient book on how to give and receive sexual pleasure. And, because of my studies, I understood well the potential that my naked body had to inflame Tzigany's desire. To dash under the sheets in modesty, I felt, would have been a miscarriage of feminine power. If he wondered how a virgin could be so well informed in the ways of love, he kept it to himself.

And so, I stood before him, holding my full breasts, in the way that the *Kama Sutra* had instructed, as if weighing melons at market. Tzigany watched with fascination, his eyes following closely my every move. I tweaked my *tetilas* gracefully, and although I understood this to be a titillating sight for a man, I had no idea just how aroused Tzigany was.

I was like a child playing with fire.

Looking down into his eyes, I wondered what he could be thinking. I was certain that he was sexually excited; for his eyes were as round as saucers, but don't forget, this being my first time, I felt a little unsure of myself: Should I go to him, or should he come to me…what should happen next? I did not know.

Studying the *Kama Sutra* was one thing, but having never put my knowledge to use, I felt somewhat apprehensive. I decided to continue arousing him; perhaps he was not quite ready. When I squeezed my breasts together, Tzigany's large eyes widened even further. He leapt out of the bed, tore off his shirt and dropped his pants and I gasped as his manhood sprang out and up like an enormous jack-in-the-box. Despite the *Kama Sutra*, I was completely unprepared for such a sight! He walked towards me, led by his member, which seemed to be urgently pointing the way.

When he wrapped his arms around me and drew me close, I felt the strong steady beat of his heart pulsing against my skin, and was keenly aware of his pene pressing urgently against my belly. Filled with curiosity, I reached down and wrapped my long fingers around it, marveling at its strength as he flexed its muscle. So this was what I had to look forward to every night of our married life. I was the luckiest wife in the world. As I squeezed, his already tight embrace became more like the embrace of a bear, making me short of breath and dizzy. The last thing I remember of the moment was the feeling of the bed under my body as I collapsed.

Yes, I fainted! Just as well, for if I were to relate any more of this story to you, I would surely bring shame upon myself, so I will leave the rest, as they say, to your imagination.

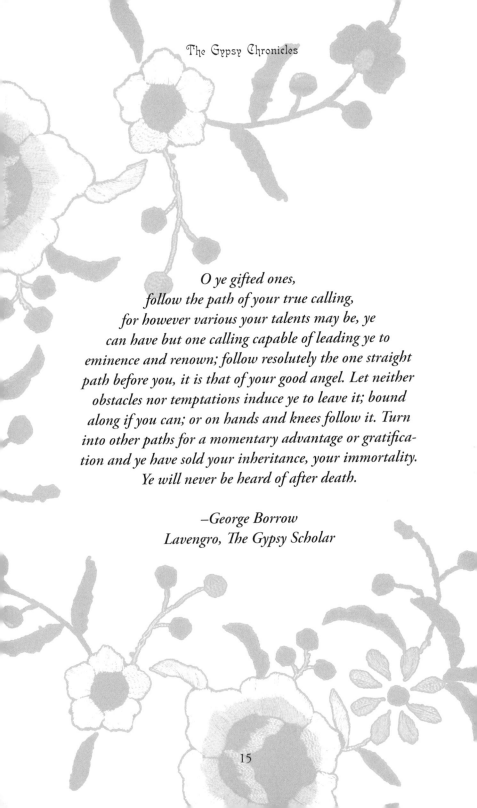

O ye gifted ones,
follow the path of your true calling,
for however various your talents may be, ye
can have but one calling capable of leading ye to
eminence and renown; follow resolutely the one straight
path before you, it is that of your good angel. Let neither
obstacles nor temptations induce ye to leave it; bound
along if you can; or on hands and knees follow it. Turn
into other paths for a momentary advantage or gratifica-
tion and ye have sold your inheritance, your immortality.
Ye will never be heard of after death.

—George Borrow
Lavengro, The Gypsy Scholar

The Business of Beds

Our first years together passed like a summer breeze. Tzigany and I took great pleasure in our marriage, and our business thrived. We chose to settle in Ronda, for Tzigany had always experienced very good luck there. Side by side we worked in his bed making studio, everyday except Sunday, making and selling Matrimonial Beds to newlyweds.

Have you heard of Ronda? It is the most the most beautiful city in all of Spain. Surrounded by mountains, the city is perched at the edge of a steep chasm that splits the town in half. The two halves face one another across the El Tajo gorge. On one side of the gorge lies the ancient Moorish quarters, and on the other, the more modern section of El Mercadillo. The Puento Nuevo bridge spans the gorge, linking old with new. Crossing it is an excitement not suitable for everyone; it is a sheer five hundred foot drop to the gushing river below!

Tzigany is not the only man enamored of this place. Ronda was Ernest Hemingway's favorite city in all of Spain. "Ronda is the perfect place if you want to bolt with someone," he wrote. "The entire background and as far as you can see is pure romance." Inspired by Ronda's dramatic scenery, Hemingway used it as a backdrop for his novel *For Whom the Bell Tolls*, where he described prisoners captured in the Spanish Civil War being thrown alive over the Puento Nuevo into the gorge.

The Austrian poet Rilke wrote, "Nothing in all of Spain is more surprising than this wild little town. I have searched the dreamed city everywhere, and at last have found it in Ronda. Come and see..."

And there is more: In Ronda you will find Spain's oldest and most beautiful bull ring – the Plaza de Torros. Charmed by its elegant old world charm, Madonna, the great American *cantaora*, filmed a musical video there some time ago, although the bull fighting aficionados in the cafes talk about it still, as though it were only yesterday.

As with any ring, more goes on at the Plaza than bull fighting alone. Twice a month it transforms itself into a giant

flea market and Gypsies from all over Andalucia are drawn to the open air of the historic ring to sell their wares. There are very good deals to be made, for those who know how to bargain. I sometimes set up a stall myself, and tell the buena ventura. Like Gypsy women everywhere I can read the future in the palm of your hand.

As a craftsman, my husband is held in very high esteem by collectors of folk art, who come to our studio from all over the world, offering great fortunes for the privilege of owning one of his unique Matrimonial Beds. Not at any price, however, will Tzigany sell to collectors, for it is the holy sanctity of marriage, the most sacred of all unions that inspires his craft, not money! He has turned down millions of dollars in his career: The currency of his imagination would be devalued in such a transaction. He is not richer who the most has, but who the least needs.

Tzigany is wary of the easy charms of wealth. He does not know, nor does he care to know, his financial worth. He presents himself to the world as a simple hard working man, for that is what he is.

With money in your pocket you are wise, you are handsome, and you sing well too, says he.

A light jingle of coin is all the cash he needs; enough for some tapas and wine at the cafe, a few cigars for his vest pocket, and a handsome tip for the little street urchin who shines his shoes every morning. Anything more is swiftly handed over to the director of finance, which is to say: Me. The vast and ever increasing sum held in our names at the Banco de Espagne would make him dizzier than the view from the Puento Nuevo.

All Tzigany requires of the world is a suitable amount of space, so that his cigar smoke may surround him in comfort. As a Gypsy he does not ask for much.

With every newlywed couple to whom he sells, his creative abilities soar, as sure as sparks fly upwards.

If he were to sell to wealthy collectors, doing so would cripple and deform the muscularity of his imagination, rendering it flaccid; abusing one's creativity always results in some kind of impotence.

It is the clean wholesome rap upon the studio door that

Tzigany welcomes most. Newlyweds! His ear is finely tuned to the particularities of their knock; an urgent rat-a-tat-tat powered by new love. For this knock only will Tzigany open the door for business. The crisp acquisitive knock of collectors, on the other hand, goes unanswered. Of course, some collectors refuse to be turned away, even though the sign on the door informs very clearly the nature of our business:

Matrimonial Beds
Sold to Newlyweds Only.
All others will be turned away.
¡Que tenga un buen día! (Have a nice day!)

Because Tzigany and I work as a team, it falls upon my shoulders to turn the collectors away. "Its nothing personal," I tell them, "its just business." I am firm with them. As a rule, the wealthier the collector, the more demanding, and therefore rude, they can be. And only when nothing else has worked, do I employ my fiercest Gypsy stare. Such a look travels deep, and never fails to draw up all manner of unnamed fear within the person at the receiving end. It is not something I enjoy doing, I assure you. While locking them hard within my gaze, I hold the fabric of my skirt at an angle, away from my body, and threaten to twitch it at them. In Spain it is well known that when Gypsy twitches her skirt in your direction, you are cursed for life, and it is only when I threaten them in this way that they retreat. Rabid collectors are the bane of our existence.

After carving the finishing touches into each bed, Tzigany turns them over to me. There is a quiet kind of magic involved in the polishing of wood, in case you did not know. In every living thing, there is a story, and wood is no exception. Oak, Mahogany, Pine…each wood has its own story locked inside the grain; a story that can be coaxed out with a vigorous rubbing of beeswax. As I polish, Tzigany takes his rest, stretching his long hard body in the soft seat in the corner. There, he smokes his cigar and watches with interest, as the beauty of the wood is reborn.

In every other country death is an ending.
Not in Spain.
Many Spaniards live indoors till the day they die,
when they are carried into the sun.
A dead man in Spain is more alive when dead
than anywhere else on earth:
his profile cuts like the edge of a barber's razor.
Tales of death and the silent contemplation
of it are familiar to Spaniards...

-Condensed version of Tony Kline's translation of
"Fredrico Garcia Lorca's Theory and Play of Duende."

Elvira Vega!

Beside our workshop, we built a fine house and looked forward to filling it with many children. However, the children were not quick in coming. I tried every trick under the sun in order to conceive, but it was no use; every turn of the tide brought with it the red sea.

Praying to God and hitting with the hammer; I used human means as though divine ones didn't exist and divine means as though human ones didn't exist.

And so it followed, that I turned to the local white witch for counsel; a wizened old crone who had stopped counting birthdays after reaching her 90th year. Her name was Elvira Vega.

Elvira wore her long white hair braided around her head like a shiny white crown, and her bright eyes had a strange intensity due to the very thick lenses of her eye-glasses that magnified her gaze three fold. Despite her great age, her body was erect and wiry, and she was in possession of great strength. She was an energetic woman who clattered about her cottage with a sure step in battered old wooden clogs.

Standing outside her open cottage door, I heard the cheerful hum of her kettle, and she beckoned me in with a slow wave of her arm.

"You look at the end of your rope," she said, noting the tightness in my shoulders.

"Very close to the end of my rope, yes."

"Sit down please Gitana, have a cuppa."

I sank into the overstuffed sofa, sighed and reached for the raspberry leaf tea which Elvira Vega offered. It was a routine we repeated each month. From her end of the sofa, a black cat stared up at me knowingly, with eyes almost human.

"I've tried every trick in the book, and still no luck," I grumbled.

"You have stood upside down on your head after sex to help the seed along?" Elvira joined me on the sofa.

"Oh yes," I sighed, weary.

"And Tzigany, he has given up those cigars, as I advised?"

"Yes, yes. Also, I add fresh nettles into my soup and rub my belly with castor oil."

Elvira sipped thoughtfully at her tea, tilting her head from one side to the other, studying me closely.

"Clear bright eyes, rosy glow in your cheeks, and glossy luster in your hair; there seems no logical reason why a healthy young woman such as yourself should not be able to conceive!"

She pushed her glasses up her nose and scratched her head.

"And Tzigany has been eating plenty of oats? This is very

important."

I nodded. "If he eats any more oats I shall have to fit him with horseshoes!"

Elvira Vega chuckled merrily and shook her head.

"Elvira, just this morning I licked the dew from every red rose bud that grows in our garden."

"Ah well. That is just an old superstition," she remarked dismissively, "but you may continue with the practice, if it makes you feel better."

"There must be something else we can try, anything?" I ventured.

She leaned toward me with dramatic intensity and whispered as though imparting a secret meant for my ears only. "There is one last thing you can try Gitana, however, if it does not work, then there is no more I can do for you. This is your last chance, and I have to warn you, it is not for the feint of heart."

I leaned forward, "What is it?"

"You are familiar with reincarnation, yes?"

"Yes…"

"Listen carefully. The constellations are aligned this evening in such a way that is favorable to luring an old soul into your womb. Comprende?"

Senora Vega leaned back in her chair and awaited my response.

I sucked in my breath and reached for the crucifix around my neck.

"This talk smacks of the occult Senora Vega!"

The old woman was direct. "Do you want a child or don't you?"

"I want a child. I do."

"Then hear me out. This morning, the body of Lucia Alvarez de Toledo was buried in the cemetery."

"Lucia Alvarez de Toledo! The *cantaora*…"

"Yes, in her day, she was a well known singer. Anyway Gitana, the planets are perfectly aligned for her reincarnation; recently expired souls are highly sensitive to the constellations. The timing is perfect. It just doesn't get any better than this. If you don't get her … somebody else will."

I leaned forward like a determined bidder at auction, "I want her!"

"Then, when the moon is high, you must pay Lucia a visit at the cemetery, and invite her into your life, as your daughter."

"I can do that," I said with confidence.

Elvira Vega held up her hand. "I am not finished Gitana. Tzigany must accompany you to the cemetery and after inviting Lucia into your lives, you and Tzigany must have sex."

"Dios mio!"

"As I said, not for the feint of heart." Elvira took a long sip of tea, observing me over the rim of her cup.

"How deviant!" I gasped, sitting back into the soft seat. "I'll do it!"

She pointed at the tea cup in my hand, "One more sip left, then we'll read the leaves."

I sipped it to the last and handed her my cup, in honor of her age and wisdom. She studied with care the pattern of tea leaves remaining at the bottom, turning the cup this way and that. Then, she widened her eyes suddenly, slapped her thigh and let out a great whooping cry of joy.

❧

I rushed home to share the good news and found Tzigany in the vegetable garden, pulling up weeds that threatened our tomato crop.

"Tzigany!" My voice resounded joy and he spun on his heels to face me.

"What is it Gitana?"

"Tzigany, we are going to have a baby!"

He felt immediately ecstatic; in addition to the usual joy a man experiences when given the news that he is to become a father, my announcement also symbolized a return to his beloved cigars. "This calls for a cigar! Where did you hide my cigars, Gitana?" He rubbed his hands together eagerly.

"No need for cigars just yet Tzigany. I'm not pregnant."

He gave a little laugh that was half a sigh and shook his head. "First you announce that we are going to have a baby, and then you tell me you are not pregnant! How am I to make sense of these conflicting statements, Gitana?"

Although I had faith in Senora Vega's graveyard scheme, I was now hesitant in sharing it with Tzigany. He would not like it, of that I was certain. Asking him to part with his cigars had been one thing, but this was another, more disturbing request which I was asking him to consider; convincing him to make love to me at the cemetery would require of him a completely open mind, and I wondered about the best way to proceed.

"We *are* going to have a baby; that much is true. We have only to *make* the baby first." But of course this was old news, and not getting to the heart of the matter at all.

Tzigany raised his brow. "We have only to *make* the baby first, you say." It sounded distinctly like an invitation to his ears, and he pulled me close, squeezing my fleshy bottom in his hands. "Right now, in the garden?"

"No, not now in the garden," I laughed. "Tonight, in the cemetery, when the moon is high..." I said it casually, in a way that froze his testiculosos and made the hair rise on his head.

At a loss for words he stared at me as I continued. "You see, according to the constellations, the time is right to lure an old soul into my womb. The 'other world' is very close during the month of May."

"Sounds suspiciously like black magic to me," Tzigany growled.

"Impossible! It came from Senora Vega and she is a white witch."

"Well then, it just sounds *loco* and I want no part of it." He turned his back to me, grabbed a rake and began to work the scattered weeds into a neat little pile.

It was the first time Tzigany had ever turned his back to me and it made my blood boil.

"It sounds *loco*? That is a bit rich coming from a man who proclaims to charm beds." I regretted the words as soon as they left my mouth, and wished I could push them back in again.

The rake fell from his hand and he turned to face me.

"I didn't mean that," I said softly.

"What did you mean?" His eyes were hard and pierced my heart.

"I meant: Do you want a child or don't you Tzigany?"

"I want a child, you know that I do." With these words,

Tzigany's expression softened, but the residue of his anger lingered, expanding the space between us.

"Then you shall have a child, but you will have to do as I ask," I said coolly, "and tonight is the night."

"When the moon is high," he said.

"When the moon is high," I repeated with a nod.

"I will think about it."

The effort we had taken to conceive a child was wearing upon our union. Until Senora Vega's strange cemetery request, it had been the absence of his beloved cigars, which Tzigany had found most difficult to bear. Every minute of every hour, his brain urged him to seek out a cigar, to fill his mouth and the air around him with the fragrant smoke from Havana. But this! Having sexual relations with his wife in a public place, a cemetery no less, was an action with which he could not easily align himself.

The remainder of the day passed in silence and our usual lighthearted laughter over dinner was replaced by deep sighs. We avoided eye contact and Tzigany ate my delicious oyster stew without commenting upon its exquisite flavor. Our alienation from one another was deeply unsettling to us both.

Tzigany felt that sex in the cemetery would be degrading to the spirits who lived there. As for me, I knew with a certainty, that of the many trials Senora Vega had put us through in order to conceive, this alone would work. But of course, it takes two to tango, and so I proceeded on the assumption that Tzigany would lend himself to the evening's strange itinerary.

After dinner, I readied myself. Over my shoulders I placed a voluminous velvet cape – my costume for the nights outing. Loosening my braids, I allowed my hair to fall in shiny waves. As Tzigany entered the room, I was standing before the mirror placing a garland of rosebuds upon my head like a crown.

"You look like a goddess," he said drawing in his breath. His first words in hours were a compliment and I took this to be a good sign. He was with me.

"Thank you." I caught his eye in the mirror and smiled.

He clapped his hands together. "So…how will we evade the watchful eye of the groundskeeper?"

"He has to sleep, just like the rest of us," I replied. I was not in the least bit worried about the groundskeeper.

"But, what if he catches us … you know…"

"You are afraid of him?"

"The one-eyed groundskeeper?" Tzigany puffed up his chest, "Please, I am not afraid of that peasant," and then added with a chuckle, "although, phantoms can cause a great fright."

"Phantoms are indeed frightening," I agreed. "I find it helps if you whistle."

Reaching for an eyebrow pencil I leaned closer to the mirror, and began to paint a beauty mark upon my right cheek.

He glanced at the beauty mark quizzically. "It's for good

luck," I explained.

"You are looking forward to this, I think…" Tzigany grinned.

The cape, the garland of rosebuds, and now this – a beauty mark. Tonight's drama was to be of Shakespearean proportions.

I reached for his hands and held them in my own, "I am looking forward to this, yes. We are going to make a baby tonight Tzigany. I can feel it in my bones."

Tzigany nodded and reached toward my cape.

"What are you wearing beneath this cape, my lovely?"

"Not now Tzigany, we don't want to dilute your passion." I stepped away.

"Gitana, surely you know by now that such a thing is not possible." He waggled his brow and advanced upon me, parting the cape dramatically, like theatre curtains. Beneath the cape, I wore a silk bodice, laced up the front. My breasts spilled over the rim which had the effect of enhancing their sensual beauty and my silk skirt opened in the center, like a tulip, leaving only a very little to the imagination. Tzigany sighed approval.

"Eres muy sexy."

I took a step back and closed the cape. "Follow me Tzigany, the moon is high."

"The moon is high, and I will follow you," he replied, entranced.

In long mystical strides, I led the way to the cemetery.

Gravestones and phantoms and love – oh my!

The full moon of the vernal equinox cast upon the gorge a strange light of penetrating intensity. The river was swollen with water due to heavy rains and roared auspiciously below. I peered over the edge of the stone bridge at the reflection of the silvery moonlight on the fast flowing river. Moonbeams danced brightly upon the broken surface of water, reflecting a clean new light back into the night. Removing a gold coin tucked inside the lining of my cape, I threw it into the void for good luck.

As luck would have it, a thick fog blanketed the cemetery grounds, concealing our presence, which suited our purpose well. We found the gravestone of Senora Lucia Alvarez de Toledo and I placed an offering of ripe pomegranates upon the earth as I summoned her spirit.

"Senora Lucia Alvarez de Toledo," I sang her name melodically into the fog, "Senora Lucia … it is I, Gitana de Torres, and I have something to ask of you."

Satisfied that the spirit of Senora Alvarez was in our midst, I pleasantly introduced her to Tzigany. I looked straight out as I spoke, as though Lucia stood right before us. Tzigany swiveled his head from me, to the space which her spirit apparently occupied. Very politely, he followed my conversation with Lucia, but did not add anything to it. It was similar to being at a party: there were the introductions, some polite chitchat, nothing heavy. I described to her the kind of life that Tzigany and I would provide for her, should she accept my invitation to be reborn into our family:

"We have a crib waiting for you Lucia, which Tzigany

has made in anticipation of your birth. You will be loved well Lucia, I promise you. And you will live in a very fine house in Ronda! Yours will be a good life…"

Satisfied that I had uttered the right words, and that my message was resonating deep within the soul of Senora Lucia, I swept my arm out to the side and preformed a deep curtsy. Tzigany followed my example with a gracious bow.

Formalities concluded, I took Tzigany by the hand and led him into the woods which bordered the cemetery.

"Oh, this is not so bad," he said lightly, as we stepped deeper into the tangle of trees.

"You didn't think we were going to do it right over her grave did you?"

"That was my impression, yes."

"Tzigany! That would be degrading to her spirit!"

"I know, I know!"

Standing within a dense circle of pines, Tzigany circled his arms around my waist.

"Your skin is burning hot, Gitana."

It was a cool evening and the fog moistened the air around us, but my skin was indeed on fire. All at once, a strange sensation came over me, such as I had never experienced before. Beneath Tzigany's hands, my body vibrated, as if the blood inside of my veins was rushing to meet with his fingertips. His hands roamed lightly over my skin, fascinated by the fine subtle pleasure he experienced through his fingertips.

Beneath his boots, the earth was fertile, the redolence of pine hung in the mist, and Tzigany de Torres knew that he was soon to be a father.

It was the mystical union of Gypsy souls, and when it

was over, we leaned against one another, returning slowly to our senses.

Tzigany laughed. "We should do this more often. What do you think, Gitana?"

It was then that I realized I was pregnant. So certain was I that a new life stirred within me that I did not bother to stand on my head to help the seed along. Instead, I pulled a cigar out of my pocket, lit it and placed it between Tzigany's lips. With pine needles clinging to the hem of my cape, and Tzigany puffing his cigar, we strolled home in the fog, arm in arm.

Dark Angel

For nine months I luxuriated in pregnancy. I loved being pregnant. Loved it! When I was hungry, I ate. When tired, I laid down to rest. And when someone knocked at the door I did not rise from my seat to answer it.

"Come in!" I shouted gaily from the soft seat in the corner as Tzigany crafted another of his beds. He raised his brow in my direction. How could it be, his looked seemed to say, that a woman who lays about all day does not have enough stored energy to answer the door properly?

The door swung open. It was Elvira Vega.

"Hola, Gitana," she said, "I have come to help you give birth."

"But I am not in labor," I replied. Indeed, although I was three weeks past my due date, the baby was in no rush to meet with the world. She kicked inside of me, a slow languid kick that rippled the length of my belly.

Elvira placed her hands upon my abdomen and closed her eyes. "I have called Doctor Urbano. He's good. The lateness of this birth troubles me Gitana."

"No Doctors," I cried. I was not enamored of hospitals.

"Do you want this baby safely delivered into this world or don't you?"

"We want a safe delivery, we do!" Tzigany and I chimed together.

"Then follow me."

As soon as I passed through the doors of the hospital, I was overcome with a strange vision of darkness that stopped me cold. Did the darkness represent death? I wondered. I did not know. I closed my eyes, confused.

The hospital smelled of disinfectant, rubbing alcohol and stale bread. It was brightly lit and filled with people rushing about in white uniforms. Behind the many doors lining either side of the long corridor were very sick people, I knew. I felt disoriented, out of my element. This was not the peaceful delivery I had envisioned.

Elvira Vega must have had some notion of what was passing through my mind. "Everything will go well," she said, assuring me with the gentle authority of a midwife. Her words had a soothing effect and strengthened my resolve. Although in a highly vulnerable state, I knew that Elvira would see me through.

And then my water broke, splashing forcefully upon the floor between my legs. My time had come, and I was promptly wheeled into a birthing chamber.

One day of painful contractions began, followed by another and yet I was no further along in my delivery than I had been at the moment I entered the hospital.

Less patient than I, Dr. Urbano suggested a special potion designed to speed things up, but I flatly refused. Then he offered to cut my belly open, reach in, and pull the baby out. The very idea of that ghastly procedure filled me with horror. No drugs, no knives; I would gut it out till the end.

Tzigany held my hand throughout, never complaining, nor indeed noticing when my fingernails broke into his skin with each contraction.

There were only two types of sensations left in the world: pain and exhaustion. I felt like something the ocean had cast upon the shoreline after a fierce storm. After each wave of contraction, I sank into a strange sleep, only to be yanked up to the surface gasping for air as another wave tore into my abdomen.

"The baby is turned the wrong way," I heard Elvira tell Tzigany.

I opened my eyes for the first time in many hours, to observe what was happening outside of my body.

Bright red blood covered the floor and I realized that the blood was my own. A janitor appeared, and with the efficient movements of one who had performed the action many times before, he plunged his mop into a bucket of hot soapy water, clearing away the blood in seconds. Did I imagine it, or did the image of a Dark Angel appear before disappearing under his mop? Fear and exhaustion, it seemed, were in cahoots and conspiring to play a nightmarish trick upon my mind.

Without warning, a tremendous contraction crashed

over me like a great tsunami of pain, washing away my last reserve of energy. The nurses busied themselves about me; their voices tense, worried.

I called out for Tzigany, but my voice sounded all wrong; as though I was calling his name from the edge of life, sounding it out over the chasm of death, and hearing its echo return from the other side.

Death was winning, I knew.

"The bleeding won't stop," I heard someone say.

"We have reason to believe she may not make it."

"Call in the priest."

Throughout this litany of death, Tzigany's voice remained by my ear; a steady hopeful whisper, "Live, Gitana. Live..."

A great shimmering light brightened the room and an angel appeared, as though through a mist. Her wings were enormous and spread out well beyond the dimensions of the room, and as she drew near, I began to experience for the world and everything in it, a deep sense of love. Hovering above the bed, she called out to me, her arms open.

When she opened her arms, the love inside of me began to vibrate at a pitch too pleasurable to maintain. My time had come, I knew, and I readied myself to leap out of my body on the count of three into heaven's sweet embrace. Limbering forward like a child filled with great daring, I began my heavenly countdown: *One ... two ....*

"Gitana, live!" Tzigany's booming voice sounded out, making an impression upon my soul. "Live, Gitana!" Make no mistake, this was no mere request on his part, but a direct order, one which reached me just as I was about to leap into the bright world beyond. I looked over my shoulder, at my lifeless body. Tzigany's great hands cradled my head, and he bent over me, insisting upon my return.

"Live!" His command was pure authority. I had no choice but to return, such was the force of his call. I would live. I would!

I recognized Father Raymundo's voice, delivering the sacrament of Extreme Unction in sonorous tones fused with the divine.

"Holy Father, physician of souls and of bodies, Who didst send Thy Only Begotten Son as the healer of every disease and our deliverer from death, heal also Thy servant Gitana de Torres from the bodily infirmity that holds her, and make her live through the grace of Christ, by the intercessions of Saint Teresa of Avila, Saint Augustine, Saint Sarah, and of all the saints."

Fortified by Father Raymundo's Holy prayers, heartened by Tzigany's command, I rallied body, mind, and soul against death. Arteries, veins and capillaries trooped together, knitting themselves up, and I felt the flow of my blood trickle to a drip.

Father Raymundo anointed my forehead with oil in the name of the Lord and Elvira rifled through her midwifery emergency bag, pulling out ointments and salves. The smell of camphor filled the air. The priest may have been performing a sacred ritual to purify my spirit before death, but Elvira was not yet ready to call it a day.

Father Raymundo turned to Elvira and addressed her in grave tones. "Your patient is very unwell and she is going to die," he informed her.

"Yes," Elvira nodded sharply, "and she's going straight to

hell."

"I have just given her extreme unction! How can you say that?"

"You have given me your medical opinion; am I not entitled to give you a religious one?"

She gave him one of her direct looks, and Father Raymundo had the odd sense that Elvira Vega was transmitting to him something he should know. Calm dignity marked her face and a strange light shone in her eye. He recognized at once that the old crone before him was aware of something he was not. And that something was that her patient was going to live. Without this knowledge she would not have cracked wise using such blasphemous words, he knew. He gave her the nod and stepped back, allowing the old doctress to attend to her patient.

Father Raymundo, Elvira and I knew the whole reckoning, but everyone else in the room, sure that I was done for, went through the motions of trying to save my life. Although I had the outwardly appearance of someone quite dead, my body was in fact turning a sharp corner in the direction of life. Elvira's winning bedside manner had served to ground me. The healing energy of delight coursed its way through my blood.

Dr. Urbano instructed the nurse to take my pulse.

"There is no pulse," she reported. My wrist dangled off the bed, lifeless, and I heard Tzigany choke back a sob.

"Feel her feet to see if they are warm," Elvira said. "If they are warm, then she's alive."

"Its true," Doctor Urbano agreed, "nobody ever died with warm feet."

"St. Teresa of Avila did!" I said, opening my eyes wide and startling everyone.

"Gitana!" Tzigany cried, his voice both incredulous and supremely happy at once.

Elvira and Father Raymundo exchanged knowing looks, whereupon he crossed himself and left the room. His job was over.

But we weren't out of the woods yet. Urbano held in his hand a three inch long hypodermic needle, readying me for surgery.

"You can put that away Doctor. The baby is on her way!" I cried out. The muscles in my belly clamped like a vice around my womb.

Elvira caught the baby, swiftly cut the umbilical cord, and passed her to Doctor Urbano.

The air was still, and except for the cheerful singing of birds outside, silent. We tensed, waiting for Angicaro to take her first breath.

Urbano held her upside down and delivered the slap of life, but there was nothing. He slapped her backside again. But again, nothing. The quiet that followed was dense, too dense. Tzigany held his breath, gasped, and then held it again, willing the baby to breathe.

Minutes passed.

Father Raymundo lingered in the doorway. Bad news has wings.

My throat tightened in fear. "Angicaro!" I shouted out, gripping the bed sheets, "Breathe my little angel! Breathe!" But Angicaro, her skin an alarming shade of blue, could not hear my shouts.

Tzigany stepped toward Dr. Urbano. Again, his voice was pure authority, "Allow me, doctor."

Puffing away at a freshly lit cigar, he leaned over Angicaro and blew a puff of smoke up her nostrils to bring her to life. At once, Angicaro coughed and let loose a piercing wail, punching at the air with tiny clenched fists.

Brimming with joy, everyone breathed a sigh of relief as she learned how to fill her lungs with air. I kissed her little face and Tzigany took a celebratory puff of his cigar.

"I am sorry, Senor Torres," the nurse said, "but I have to ask you to put out the cigar. It is against safety regulations to smoke in a hospital."

Taking one last puff, he watched Angicaro wave her tiny hands in smoky air. "Even so," he said, " where there are angels, there must also be clouds."

Don't you believe that there is in man,
a deep so profound,
as to be hidden even to him in who it is?

– Saint Augustine

Raguel:
The Heartbreaking Story
of a 'Fallen Angel'

Raguel Rodriguez was seven years old when he noticed an unusual plant growing in his neighbor's garden. The plant interested him, and he tracked the progression of its gradual ripening, daily. Kiwi vines were new to Spain and so only a very few gardens had them. They were rare and therefore valuable; like gold or diamonds, Raguel thought, imagining the emerald greenness beneath the skin's surface.

The day soon came when the vines were heavy with ripe fruit. Raguel had never tasted a kiwi before, and so he felt a strange yearning. Pressing his nose against the window, the young boy stared, entranced, as the wind moved through the branches of the kiwi vine, summoning him forward, with a wave.

Once outside, he took small steps in the direction of the vine and little by little found himself seated comfortably in its cool shade. Looking up, he studied the fruit dangling over head and found it to be beautiful, for it had a delicate forest of soft stubble on its skin like his father's unshaven face in the morning.

He stroked the stubbly skin with his fingers, delicately, and felt it to be good, so he tugged at the fruit gently; not to pick it, he told himself, but just to get a feel for the resistance.

However, the fruit yielded, and so Raguel pulled it away from the branch. It felt good in his hand, this rare fruit, and he caressed it in an almost loving way. Holding it between his thumb and his forefinger he held it out against the blue sky, turning it this way and that before sinking his teeth into its flavorful green interior. With his eyes closed, he treasured the taste in his mouth, one bite after another, until there was nothing left of the fruit but the stem.

Raguel licked his lips. Rare fruits were delicious, he thought, but one was not enough, and so he reached for a second. Having finished the second fruit, he found that he could not stop, and so he ate another, and another and another. The more he ate, the more he wanted and he reasoned that his crime would go undetected, for his neighbor was so thick in the head that he could speak without moving his brain, and would surely not notice that some of his precious fruit had gone missing.

There remained one last kiwi on the vine, and Raguel would have eaten that one also, if a sudden pain had not seized upon his belly. Overfull and unable to move, he curled his body into the shape of a ball. Moaning in pain and clutching at his bloated belly, his father found him beneath the vine and realized at once what Raguel had done. Ignacio then gathered his son up into his strong arms and carried him home.

A devout man of faith, Ignacio was deeply ashamed of his son's actions and was determined to pluck the weed of sin from his soul before it had a chance to sink deeper roots. Towards this end, he chose his words with great care.

"Sin separates man from God, and this is a terrible thing," he began. Raguel nodded in agreement, but did not seem suitably moved, leaving Ignacio to conclude that his son's commitment to God was weak. To put the fear of God into him, he told Raguel about fallen angels; surely this would set his son on the straight and narrow path.

"Fallen angels are dark beings who do not return God's love," began Ignacio. "They are under Satan's command and occupy the souls of unbelievers, making them do sinful things … like stealing kiwis."

The image of a fallen angel in command of his soul, blazed within the young boy's imagination. Such talk terrified Raguel, as his father knew well that it would.

"But father, I am a believer, I am! I am!" Raguel rubbed into his teary eyes with his fists and sobbed. His father seemed to be suggesting that he was a fallen angel and therefore more at one with Satan, than with God. The idea of a fallen angel in possession of his soul filled Raguel with horror and a hot flush of panic surged through him.

Ignacio could see that his words were having the desired effect and so he continued, "If your mother were alive this would break her heart," he said wistfully, shaking his head.

At the mention of his mother, who had had died while giving birth, Raguel's world filled with blackness. His head became heavy and sank into his chest. Wounded deeply, he fell to the ground, prostrate in his loneliness. The dark wings of a fallen angel beat overhead. Raguel's soul was bleeding, and he could cry no more.

Ignacio brought his broken son onto his lap and embraced him tenderly, certain that his carefully aimed words had reached their mark. The fear of God is potent in exterminating sin, he knew.

"Tomorrow you will confess your sins in Church my son, and all will be well," he informed Raguel, and believed it to be so.

But it was not so. For, when Raguel Gutierrez grew up, he became a highly enterprising entrepreneur in crime.

From silly devotions and from sour-faced saints, good Lord, deliver us.

–St. Teresa of Avila

Angicaro

The years passed and it became increasingly apparent that a divine presence was dwelling within our home, for Angicaro was truly an angel. One had only to listen to her voice to feel the presence of God. When she sang, flowers came into bloom and little birds tilted their heads to one side, marveling at her sparkling delivery.

Her great talent eventually came to the attention of recording companies, who offered her great sums of money to sing for them alone. Unlike Lucia Alvarez de Toledo however, fame and fortune did not interest Angicaro, for she was already living in the light of eternity: The higher path of her true calling was devoted to God.

Coming from the fire of a heart overflowing with love, Angicaro's prayers, which she was in the habit of singing aloud, nourished and expanded the luminosity of her soul. God's love shone through her and wherever she went, people reached out to touch her. It was said she was treading the path of sainthood.

Little by little, deepened through the practice of prayer,

it came to light that she had the ability to turn souls, and eighteen years after the day she was born, she was all set to marry Jesus Christ – to become a nun at Ronda's Merced Carmelite Convent, but that was before another great love appeared on the scene ...

Raguel and Angicaro

I was breathing away the foggy mists of sleep that clung to my body after a particularly long siesta, stretching lazily in my big wonderful bed, when Angicaro tiptoed into the room and lay down beside me. Tzigany had already left to return to work, and so we were quite alone. I sensed a mother-daughter chat coming on.

"Que pasa Angicaro?"

There was something peculiar in her aspect. Although she lay beside me, she was a million miles away.

"Angicaaaaaro," I sang out lightly, "I speak to you, but you do not answer."

She smiled.

"I've met a diamond thief, Mama."

"And has he stolen your heart?" I guessed, crossing my fingers that it was not so.

She faced my way, looking me in the eye. "You cannot steal that which already belongs to you."

Well!

To my credit, I did not bat an eye. I find it best not to

pass judgment on matters of the heart, even if the heart in question belongs to your own daughter. That is not to say I was not without reservation: At the end of the day, a diamond thief is still a diamond thief.

"But it was my understanding that your heart belongs to Jesus."

Angicaro sighed. "I can't marry both Jesus Christ and Raguel Rodriguez; however I can marry Raguel, and still have Jesus in my heart."

At this news, my eyes betrayed me, and I blinked with force. Had I heard correctly? Angicaro was breaking off her engagement with Jesus Christ in favor of marrying a diamond thief?

"So, my daughter is marrying a diamond thief."

She gave me a chummy wink. "Don't worry mama, I'll turn him around in no time. You will see!"

Her absolute self confidence caught me up short, until I remembered how well connected she is. How could I forget? Through Angicaro, God magnifies his light. The diamond thief did not stand a chance. His dark shadows would be dispelled in no time. I smiled and brushed lightly the back of my hand against her cheek.

"Oh. I'm not worried Angicaro." If anyone could turn a thief around, it was she.

Still, she was marrying a diamond thief, ay yi yi. This was more than just an interesting turn of events.

"Please don't share with papa what I have told you about Raguel's career. His faith in my ability does not match yours. The less he knows the better."

I nodded in agreement. It does happen sometimes, that

the less Tzigany knows, the better. That said, I knew he would be quick to discern Raguel's true nature on his own.

"So tell me, how did you meet Raguel?"

"I met him on the bus." In recounting the event, Angicaro's eyes shone. "There was but one seat left and that seat was next to him."

Is there no better story, than the story of how one comes to meet the great love of one's life? I think not. I let my head sink back into the pillow.

"Give me the whole reckoning."

I closed my eyes so that Angicaro's tale could play out upon the great movie screen of my imagination: Upon the screen I saw Raguel, the handsome diamond thief, sitting in the back row of the bus, watching Angicaro as she searched for a seat.

Greeting the Angel

Hers was a kaleidoscopic beauty; every little move she made brought attention to one aspect or another of her charms. Lifting her chin as she searched for a seat, Raguel could not but notice the graceful line of her neck; and when she turned, the profile of a Roman princess appeared. He waited patiently for the beauty to discover that the last empty seat was next to him.

When she lowered herself into the seat, her bare knee brushed lightly against his. Turning with interest in her direction, Raguel was surprised to find that her amber eyes were already fixed upon his, and that they were filled with as much curiosity as his own.

"Hello my friend." Her raspy voice was sweet and low. "I am Angicaro."

She reached out to shake Raguel's hand and the smell of beeswax teased at his nostrils. She smelled of church candles! And so he breathed her in again.

Raguel was disarmed by her frank and open warmth, and confused by a strange new feeling rattling away inside of his heart. The message inside Angicaro's golden gaze traveled upon the tip of a well aimed arrow, and piercing his heart, caused within him a stab of pleasure so profound that he wished for it never to end. Deeply moved, but not knowing why, he experienced a strange yearning to press his head against her breast, and weep. For the very first time in his life, the diamond thief felt at home.

As Angicaro turned her attention away from him, Raguel felt a pang and tried to think of something clever to say in order to regain her attention. He was just about to speak when she touched his arm and nodded with concern toward the front of the bus, where a rowdy gang of delinquents were clambering aboard.

They were rough in their manner. The leader was a mean looking fellow who strolled down the aisle with a self-satisfied bravado. Raguel did not care for the appearance of the approaching rabble, and readied himself for confrontation.

Stopping before a group of elderly men, the gang leader looked down at them, eyeing them in a way which made clear his intention: He wanted their seats.

Although old, the men were steadfast, and returned the

gang leader's look with a look of their own: We realize you want our seats; their eyes seemed to say, but please understand that we are old and tired, and it is therefore our wish to remain seated.

One of the gang, a broad beamed young woman with badly colored hair, wailed at the old men, "Give us your seats! Now!"

The bus driver looked into his surveillance mirror, apprehensive. Raguel's hands itched and his muscles coiled. Leaning forward, he readied himself to deal with the gang, but he was too slow, for someone else had already stolen his thunder.

And that somebody was Angicaro.

Watching the scene unfold, Angicaro found herself within the embrace of an idea, and opened her mouth to sing. Her voice was rich and fulsome and she waggled her brows at Raguel, beckoning him to join her in song. At once, he too began to sing, and their voices came together in the well loved Spanish folk song, 'De Colores,' a song that means that when your soul is full of grace, it is as beautiful as a springtime meadow in full bloom. Whenever this song is sung, people join hands and sway, and so Angicaro took Raguel's hand in hers, and together they swayed in song.

De Colores,
We witness the sun upon
clear and bright mornings.

The gang leader shot Angicaro and Raguel a hard look full of menace, but within seconds the well known song traveled the length of the bus like a powerful tide, pulling everyone into its warm current. Bound together in spirit, every passenger was singing the song!

De colores,
The fields like to dress in all colors
during the springtime!

As the cheerful tune resounded in the gang leader's ears, he felt a growing sense of unease. It was clearly not his day. He could either sing, or he could get off the bus, but he would most certainly not be sitting down. The two elderly men seated beneath him held hands, swaying in song. Would the gang leader sing also? All eyes on the bus locked upon him, curious to see what he would next do.

De Colores,
The sun gives the treasure
of God's light to His children.

Powered by the joyful singing, a big happy wave washed over the gang leader's spirit, knocking his sneering attitude right out from beneath him. What else could he do, but take a very deep breath, and sing? And of course, this is what he did, and with great feeling too!

De colores,
The diamond will sparkle
when brought to the light.

As the gang leader sang, so too did his gang, causing an ever stronger swell of joy to surge throughout. Angicaro turned towards Raguel and squeezed his hand. It was her stop. Rising from her seat, she led him off of the bus, and into her life.

> *And so must all love*
> *be of many bright colors,*
> *to make my heart cry!*

"De Colores" traveled deep into the hearts of all the passengers of the bus that day. New passengers, at first taken aback, soon joined in, and departing passengers carried the song into the crowded streets, until all of Ronda was in song. Olé!

"What a beautiful story!" I cried, bringing my hands together.

"But wait, there's more!" Angicaro whispered with great excitement. "Raguel is not yet aware that I know he is a diamond thief!"

"Go on ..."

Drawing a deep breath, Angicaro commenced to tell me the story of how she discovered Raguel's dark secret.

After stepping off the bus, Angicaro took her beloved to the place she loved best.

As it was confession time, and the Iglesias de Santa Maria quite empty, Raguel moved towards the confessional chamber. "This is going to take a while," he informed her.

He passed Angicaro his back pack, suggesting that she help herself to an apple within. Taking the pack, Angicaro headed for the garden sanctuary. However, when she reached inside to help herself to an apple, what she found was a cache of diamonds wrapped in newspaper instead. And upon the newspaper in which the diamonds were wrapped, was printed the story of their provenance: "Diamond Thief is Spain's Greatest Rascal!" The headline exclaimed. Angicaro raised her brows in surprise, and read the article.

Raguel's taking was a cache of diamonds valued in the millions. With no clues to work from, no leads to follow, and not a single clue as to the identity of the thief, police detectives all over Spain were plodding a very cold path.

Angicaro wrapped the diamonds in the newspaper and carefully returned them to the pack. Apparently, the man in the confessional chamber, was a thief of the first water! But why would such a professional so carelessly hand to a complete stranger, his cache of diamonds?

Putting one and one together, Angicaro quickly summed up the sin to which Raguel was confessing.

Only one other person in all of Spain knew the identity of the infamous jewel thief and he wasn't talking. How could he? He was a priest and therefore, bound to secrecy; all words spoken within the confessional, are for God's ears only, and travel no further.

The priest considered the thief before him: Raguel was a handsome man in possession of a quiet intelligence and a heartbreakingly beautiful gaze; both of which he hid behind long drooping eyelashes and a soft spoken voice. Tall and manly, he had an athletic grace and was well mannered in every way. The priest could not but marvel at how such a gifted young man could bitch his talents to thievery.

"Why is it that you rob jewelry stores?" Father Raymundo asked.

Raguel shrugged. "Because, that is where the diamonds are." He did not know the deeper reason why.

"Return the diamonds and all will be forgiven."

"I will return them," replied Raguel, observing how his lie pleased the priest.

Ronda was to be a fresh start for Raguel. He was a modern man in search of his soul. The latest newspaper reports had carried mythical stories about him, hailing him as 'Spain's Greatest Rascal.' And as he read those stories, it began to feel as though what he was, was what he was meant to be. However, the shadow of his guilt continued to play its burdensome role and so he had entered into confession with great hope.

After his confession, Raguel felt better: He found himself to be sinful, but not guilty, and so, despite his promise to the priest, he allowed himself a few weeks respite, in order to consider more fully his next move.

He stepped into the garden sanctuary and Angicaro

greeted him with a smile so radiant it stopped him short in his step. No ordinary smile, it was more a glimpse of the divine. So dazzled was he by what he saw, that he stood still for quite some time inside of her gaze.

Greeting the Snake

With a dozen white roses for Angicaro, Raguel knocked upon the door of our house. When the door swung open and Tzigany appeared, Raguel instinctively took a step back.

"I am Angicaro's father," Tzigany said, extending his hand in greeting.

The force behind Tzigany's steady gaze set Raguel off balance, and he blinked several times before offering his hand in return.

"Greetings Senor Torres, I am honored to make your acquaintance. I am Raguel Rodriguez."

"Then I suppose you had better come in, Raguel," Tzigany suggested, in crisp even tones.

Raguel offered a formal bow and Tzigany turned, leading him to the interior patio. Water splashed cheerfully in the fountain, jasmine plants scented the air and Tzigany and Raguel faced one another, in silence. Lighting a cigar, Tzigany eyed the young man who was claiming his daughter's affections. There was something in Raguel which he did not warm to. In his mind's eye, there flashed the image of a snake. Tzigany did not care for snakes, but assuming some degree of courtesy, he offered the snake a cigar.

"No thank you, I don't smoke."

"You don't have to smoke to enjoy a cigar," Tzigany said gruffly, blowing smoke into Raguel's face.

Raguel fought the urge to wave the smoke away, and nodded agreeably.

As for my part, I followed their conversation with some amusement. Sitting quietly, I puffed mildly on the cigar which Tzigany had offered to me.

"How do you earn your living?" Tzigany asked.

Raguel looked away briefly, before answering. "I am a businessman."

Tzigany's eyes narrowed, "Is that so?" An image of dirty coins flashed through his mind: Thievery would be more like it, he figured, and he blew smoke into the thief's face. "A businessman, you say." His voice did not conceal his disbelief.

"It is the truth and no lie, brother." Raguel said softly. Tzigany was onto him, he knew.

Raguel lowered his long lashes over his eyes, but when he raised them, Tzigany's eyes were still fixed upon him; intense, all knowing.

"Raguel Rodriguez! Businessman my ass," Tzigany brooded after Angicaro and Raguel had departed for the cinema. "That man lies like the wind of make-believe. He is a lying, thieving snake and not suitable for our daughter!"

"Angicaro is precisely what a man like Raguel needs. She'll turn him around in no time, you will see." I knew what I knew.

Tzigany could see everything before him with 20/20 vision, however, when it came to the future, he was utterly blind. I shook my head at his shortsightedness and urged him not to worry, but it was no good, he held on to the present day as though tomorrow did not exist. Gah!

"I knew all that goodness of hers would land her into trouble one day," he lamented.

I rolled my eyes. "Tzigany, did you not notice Raguel pulling all the thorns off the stems of the roses before handing them to Angicaro?" My voice aligned deep significance to his action.

"And what does this foretell?" He frowned, baffled.

I sighed at having to explain the obvious. "Raguel does not wish to harm Angicaro. He pulled the thorns off the roses so that they would not pierce her skin. He is protective towards her, and this is a very good sign!"

"No Gitana. The reason Raguel pulled the thorns off the roses, is because I make him very nervous!"

"This is also true," I chuckled.

Tzigany battled with the voices of two minds as he constructed a Matrimonial Bed for Angicaro and Raguel. As much as he would have liked to ban Raguel from their lives, the larger part of him longed to take joy in his daughter's marriage and so, despite his instinctive distrust of Raguel, the bed was outstanding when completed; the double doves nesting inside a giant heart stood out most handsomely on the headboard.

Raguel had a discerning eye for rare things. He could immediately tell a master's painting from a valueless fraud, or a diamond from cut crystal, and so when he gazed upon the Matrimonial Bed which Tzigany had made, he recognized it for what it was: A rare and beautiful masterpiece. He drew in his breath, marveling at the grand dimensions, fascinated by the magical curves carved so perfectly into the wood. The four posters stood like elegant towers, proudly framing the bed beneath a magnificent canopy. The duvet, covered in velvet damask, featured a richly textured Moorish pattern in shades of pale gold and creamy white, while the matching drapery was lined in silk and tied back at the posts with a ball tassel. It was altogether lovely. An arrangement of pillows of all shapes and sizes beneath the headboard provided the finishing touch: There was a damask pillow with bullion fringe, several paisley patterned ones with allover tassels, and an embroidered pillow in velvet edged in gold rouche. In a bed such as this, with Angicaro by his side, Raguel would feel like a king!

Of course, one can not stand before such a bed, potently charmed as it is, without the imagination eventually asserting itself, and so, in his mind's eye there blazed an image of Angicaro reclining elegantly upon the silken pile of pillows in the center of the bed, naked as the day she was born, beckoning him to join her. Raguel began to swell with the sweet ache of pleasure and his blood suffused with heat. The bed Tzigany had made was a bed like no other.

He turned to face his future father in law, offering him

his heart felt thanks.

Tzigany shrugged and blew cigar smoke into Raguel's face.

I have phrases and whole pages memorized,
but nothing can be told of love.

You must wait until you and I
are living together.

In the conversation we'll have
then ... be patient ... then.

—Coleman Barks; Rumi

Secrets

On their wedding night, Raguel lay upon the magnificent bed, brimming with desire for Angicaro. The sheer white fabric of her negligee was so thin that he could see clearly the rosy aureoles of her full breasts, the curve of her hips, and the dark hair of her *pudenda* beneath.

"Angicaro…" He breathed her name. His life was about to become the enactment of his dreams and innermost fantasies.

"Before we make love, I'd like to tell you a secret."

"Then tell me your secret, but be quick," he whispered, biting her neck gently.

She whispered into his ear, "Before you Raguel, there was another man."

"Say no more," he closed his eyes. "I do not wish to know."

No sooner had he closed his eyes but he opened them again. "Anyone I know?"

"Oh yes, I'm sure you know him. He is the most famous man in the world, and I was engaged to marry him."

Raguel shook his head, why was she telling him this now, on their wedding night?

"Tell me his name."

"His name is Jesus. Jesus Christ."

Raguel gasped. "You mean you were going to become a nun?" This surprised him, and yet…

"Yes, I was going to marry Jesus, but I chose you instead."

"I hope that I am worthy of your love," he murmured,

his eyes downcast. The other man was not just any other man, but Jesus Christ. *The* Man.

"You are absolutely worthy of my love Raguel."

"Why did you choose me over him?"

"Jesus is a very demanding husband!" She laughed fruitily. "You are by far the easier choice."

He held her hand, staring at the pink diamond engagement ring upon her finger; a stolen diamond. She deserved better.

"I told you my secret, now you must tell me yours."

Raguel lowered his lashes, "I have no secret."

"Everyone has a secret," she persisted.

He shrugged, "Truly, I have no secret." He reached to pull her close, but she drew back sharply.

"You mean to tell me that 'Spain's Greatest Rascal' has no secret?"

She'd obviously been reading the papers, but how did she figure out it was him? Eyeing him with the same fixed gaze of her father, Angicaro drew out his truth.

"You are a rascal indeed," she whispered.

The heat of shame coursed its way through Raguel's blood. He was disgraced and suddenly alone; a fallen angel rejected first by God and now, he was sure, by Angicaro.

"How did you find out?"

"Before confession, you handed me your back pack and suggested I help myself to an apple. But what I found instead, were stolen diamonds wrapped inside a newspaper article that told me the whole story."

Raguel frowned. "You have known since then? And still you married me?" There was no logic in what she was telling him. Surely, knowing him to be a thief, she should have cancelled the wedding.

"Of course I still married you Raguel. Do you think I am so proud that I would merely glance at you while you are in need? That I would turn my back and continue on my way?" She looked at the back pack in the corner; the diamonds were still inside, she knew.

Although a thief and therefore a sinner, Raguel's mind was still very much alive to the workings of the Holy Spirit. That his betrayal did not blind Angicaro to his pain was an indication that the Holy Spirit dwelled firmly within her soul.

"What thief worth his salt hides diamonds in a knapsack where they can be so easily found? Clearly, Raguel, on some level you wished for me to discover them!"

It was a compelling logic and Raguel realized that he was only beginning to understand her beautiful heart. Angicaro was incandescent with the Holy Spirit, and her luminosity dazzled him more than any of his diamonds.

"You've known all of this for a week, and yet you waited until our wedding night to tell me. Why?"

She raised her gown over her head and dropped it to the floor. Her skin was ripe and lush and Raguel longed to taste her but dared not. Not yet. Her steady gaze fell upon him in such a way that made it clear for the time being, he was only to look. "I waited until our wedding night Raguel, because I want to make a deal with you."

His voice was thick and low. "I am in the mood to bargain." Angicaro's heat passed through the sheets, and he felt the soft magnetic pull of her femininity.

She pulled the diamond ring from her finger and tossed

it over her shoulder. It clattered to the floor.

"You have a decision to make, Raguel. It's either me or the diamonds. You can't have both … Are you with me?"

"I am with you," he said without hesitation. "You are all the treasure I need."

His words pleased her better than any other he could have spoken at that moment, and she fell with delight into his arms, allowing herself to burn with love's heat. Her look to him was wholly on fire and although she lay becalmed inside his tender embrace, she experienced the sensation of movement; a pleasurable stirring in the central mansion of her soul.

Her kisses were like a rich blessing, enkindling within him a bonfire of heavenly sensation. Their's was a romance of loving glances, ecstasy and sweet words. She called his name, and he whispered back: *I am yours.*

Like a blossom she opened up to him, and he settled upon her innocence like a delicate mist, basking in their union.

What greater love can there be than this, Raguel wondered, reaching a dizzying state, losing himself.

Dazed and tranquil, the two lovebirds fell asleep, nesting in the boughs of the other's soul. Beside their bed, upon the old wooden bureau, a moth darted, drawn, and drawn again, into the flame of a candle.

At first light, Spain's Greatest Rascal packed up the diamonds to return them to their rightful owner. The slow turning of his soul had come full circle: He was brand new.

Opening wide the wooden shutters of the balcony, the slant of the morning sun fell upon his cold toes, warming them. Looking down, he found his toes to be beautiful and he wiggled them in the sunlight, amused by the fine dark hair that grew upon the knuckles.

The world and everything in it leaves a trace, like a second message in its passing. An echo. Standing in the warm beams of light, Raguel felt God's love echo deeply throughout his soul – he was awake to God as never before.

Leveling his head to the sun in meditation, he closed his eyes and opened his heart. And as morning light filled the sky, Raguel expanded, redefining his feelings of love for Angicaro. The best years of his life were about to begin, he knew.

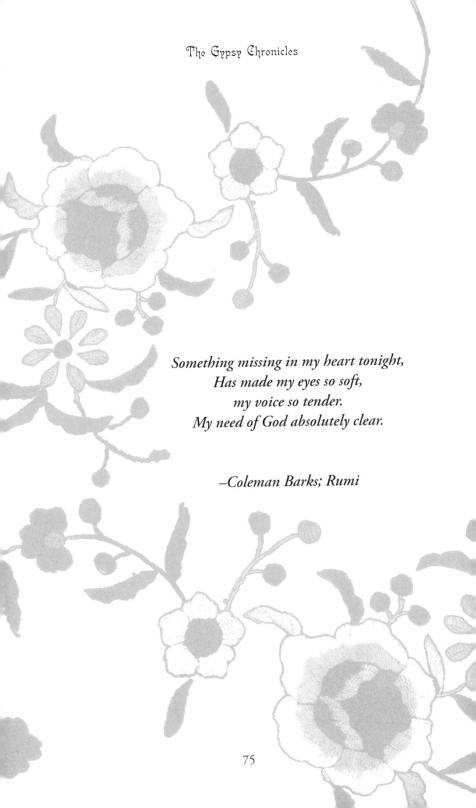

Something missing in my heart tonight,
Has made my eyes so soft,
my voice so tender.
My need of God absolutely clear.

—Coleman Barks; Rumi

Don't surrender your loneliness
so quickly. Let it cut more deep.
Let it ferment and season you,
As few human or divine ingredients can.

–Coleman Barks; Rumi

The Gypsy Chronicles

Estrella de la Flamenca

Ask me questions. Question me. Ask. There must be a little sign posted above my head with these very words printed upon it, for I get more than my share of questions.

I wonder sometimes, how it came to pass that I should be considered an authority on matters of the heart. Could it be because my husband carves charming love birds into the headboards of his Matrimonial Beds? But never mind, it does not matter. I am in the full bloom of my age, with forty five years and what use a fully ripened wisdom, if not to share? We grow into our prime to guide others along roads we have already passed.

I serve the young women of the barrio faithfully, whenever asked. Here is where I am, and here is where they come – to my little table, the one against the sunny wall outside La Café de la Alegria, the place of many a womanly chat. *Café con leche'*, some sugary *churros*, and a little heart to heart with Gitana.

And while it is true that I know a thing or two about matters of the heart, I certainly do not have all the answers. More often than not, all that is required is that I be a good ear: The word is silver, silence gold, and sometimes, the best word is the one not said. This was one of those times.

"Where is he Gitana?"

"Where is whom, Estrella?"

"The great love of my life, of course. Ten years I have been waiting, and still he has not revealed his identity. I'm getting impatient!"

Estrella stomped her foot. Then she stomped the other foot. Three times. Let me explain: Estrella is a flamenco dancer who does not save her performances for the stage alone.

"Who is he? When is he coming, and what is taking him so long?" Estrella asked, dunking her churros deep into her café con leche'.

"Perhaps you will meet him tonight," I suggested. It could happen.

In these fast moving times of change in which we live, it is rare to find a woman with twenty seven years of age, who is still a virgin. But a virgin is what Estrella was, and a virgin Estrella would remain until her wedding night, as most Gypsy women worth their salt usually are. She was waiting for the right man, for her husband. Lately, however, Estrella was alarmed by the ams of the clock, which seemed to be rotating at an increasingly faster pace.

It was not for lack of suitors that Estrella found herself alone in the world. Suitors were as familiar to Estrella as her own shadow. After a performance, if every man in the audience did not wish to make love to her, then the performance was not a success in Estrella's opinion. But Estrella never failed.

She soared above the expectations of her audience and had numerous admirers. It was just finding the right one that presented the problem.

I leaned back into my chair to observe her as she spoke. The little golden mirrors sewn into her shawl reflected sunlight into her amber eyes, so that they appeared to be glowing from within. She cut such an interesting figure that small children rushed up to our table just to touch the hem of her skirt for good luck, as though she were a talisman and in possession of great magic. And although it could not be said that Estrella de la Flamenca was fashionable, she certainly had a style all her own, so much so that the trendsetting women of the street turned their heads in her direction, fascinated by her splendid bearing. Estrella was impressive to behold.

Gold was her element. The hoops that dangled from her ears, the chains around her neck, her rings and many bracelets – all of these pieces were of gold. Even her front incisor was capped in gold, and shone against her white even teeth whenever she smiled. But Estrella did not smile very often. Not lately, anyway. She was frustrated. Estrella needed a man!

Leaning back into her chair, she crossed her legs and rotated her foot at the ankle. As always, she was wearing professional flamenco shoes, the kind with a single elastic strap across the instep and nails driven into the heels. Giving me one of her direct looks, she said, "You can imagine in what state I am."

"I can indeed." I touched lightly the small vase of daisies upon the table while Estrella's fingers touched the other side, and between us, we pushed it back and forth absentmindedly as we conversed.

She felt that a strange force was exerting its will upon her life, one which prevented her from finding love, and yet she also viewed her situation as a test; one which she was determined not to fail. "I am caught between the sword and the wall," she said. But the tension served her well, for with it she was able to translate raw emotion into brilliant performances. Lowering her head, she steeled herself against temptation: An aging virgin? Perhaps so, however, Estrella de la Flamenca would not settle for anything less than just the right man.

Alone in the world, she found that she had endurance and courage, and that she could wait out time. Not one to surrender to loneliness, she allowed it to cut into, ferment and season her. When it came to love, better alone than poorly accompanied, Estrella reasoned. One day her husband would reveal himself. Until then, she had her dance and the love of her loyal fans.

One never knew what to expect with Estrella de la Flamenca, and of course, this was part of her great magic! I remember the time she reached over before a performance and borrowed Tzigany's cigar. Working her skirt with one hand and waving the cigar like a wand with the other, she claimed possession of the stage. Everyone watched, mesmerized as she brought the cigar slowly to her mouth, inhaled its smoke, and blew it out of her ears! Where there is smoke, there is Estrella!

So Estrella came, Estrella danced and Estrella left alone, and we all made allowances. We watched her lean against her solitude, giving shape to her loneliness by dancing against the heft of it. Pressing her body neatly into its weighty contours, she tore at it with long elegant fingers, as though it were mere wallpaper she could remove at will.

The sureness of her movements and sexual energy attached to them invited immediate response. Every man felt that he alone possessed the power to soothe her soul.

Alone in her bed at night, she would draw her pillow close. She wanted to feel something good – but with no man, there was nothing to feel. Nothing was good. And so she wanted nothing. How could this be, she wondered, wrapping her arms around the pillow, that I am excited over nothing? Nothing excites me.

Some mornings, to cheer herself up, she would imagine her future husband asleep beside her in the bed. Pretending they were awakening together, she would think: I am here, you are there, and we are here – together. Sometimes it was he who reached for the morning's first squeeze, other times she – but it was always he who prepared the coffee, for she was lazy in the morning. Undercover of rumpled sheets, she would dream-gaze into the sunrise while the steam rose, curling into happy smiles all around.

He was home at last ... or so she liked to imagine.

Her soul itched. She took to shouting out during performances. Such vocal behavior in a dancer was unprecedented. "Where is he?!" She would cry out in her raspy voice. There was no tempering this artist. Her soul itched and so she scratched it. Her lips burned to call out the name of her husband. "I am waiting for you! *Andelez!*"

Estrella wore no stockings when she danced and she

wore her long hair loose, so that it could move with her as she danced. Lately, she had taken to kicking her shoes off into the crowd after performances. Perhaps she hoped that they would land in the lap of Prince Charming. It could happen.

She transmitted a sensibility of strength and as a result, her fans never tired of her delivery. The connection they experienced through her was addictive and she always left them in want of more. An invisible bridge linked her heart with theirs, and through her, they experienced transcendence. It was a shared journey. Many of her fans had tears in their eyes during her performances, but knew not why they cried. And so strong was Estrella's connection to them, that the mere sight of her, even passing by on the street, could trigger an emotional response.

Estrella's last suitor had been a museum curator by the name of Domingo. Shocked after one of her more daring soul baring performances, he berated her in front of her adoring crowd: "You might as well be naked up there, exposing your feelings in the way that you do! Have you no shame?"

The room fell silent and Estrella's fans dropped their jaws. How dare he say these things to her? As one, they turned their heads from Domingo to Estrella, ready to lend her their support.

She cast upon him a withering look, and twitched her skirt in his direction. Domingo was not the man for her, clearly, and was ready for the boot. Gathering all around, the fans closed ranks upon him, forcing him to back slowly out of the café.

"What's happening?" The bewildered curator shouted

over their heads.

Estrella knocked on the counter of the bar and a glass of red wine appeared before her. She rolled her eyes at Domingo, still awaiting her response, although it was fairly obvious to all that she no longer wanted anything more to do with him.

"What's happening," she explained wearily, "is that I never wish to meet with you on this side of the grave." If the curator could not understand the beauty of her craft – if he was insulted by the emotion she invested in her moves, then he did not value her and she was better off without him.

"*Vaya!* Never return to this place! It belongs to Estrella alone!" went the shouts of her fans.

After the door closed behind him, Estrella shrugged her shoulders. "Drama if I dance, drama if I do not. What am I going to do?"

"Dance!" the crowd shouted.

Estrella took a healthy sip of her wine and raised her glass high, "To my good friends! All of you!"

Father Raymundo, man of God first and Flamenco aficionado second, never missed a single of Estrella's performances. Quietly, he made his way towards her and took her aside. He had information of great import which he wished to share with her alone.

In hushed tones, he described to Estrella a vision that had appeared to him while warming his hands before a wire coiled heater.

"Do you mean the type of heater which sits upon the floor and gives off glowing red coils of heat?" Estrella asked with interest.

"The same," Father Raymundo affirmed. "Anyway, I was

warming my hands before the heater, when all of a sudden the glowing coils seemed to rearrange themselves into the image of you…" and here Father Raymundo paused, barely able to contain his excitement, "and your future husband! The two of you appeared, surrounded by a heart, in those glowing red coils of heat."

Estrella's heart skipped a beat and her breath caught. "You had a vision of my future husband?!"

Father Raymundo pursed his lips together into a humble smile. "Indeed I did. Have faith Estrella, he is on his way!"

"But when is he due?" Estrella leaned forward.

"That, I cannot say. However, I do know that I shall be present to witness his arrival," and here he leaned forward and their heads met over the small round table.

"Estrella, I want you to know that I am always prepared to conduct the wedding ceremony – just like that!" He snapped his fingers over his head.

And so, heartened by Father Raymundo's vision, Estrella never lost faith. Be that as it may, the nights alone were many and long, and at bed time Estrella had visions of her own. Although she had never made love to a man, she could imagine what her first time might feel like: She would take him by the hand, and then by his other hand. This is what she had in her mind. And if his hands felt right, and she knew that they would, she would draw him close. Close by and closer still, she would come to know him slowly – by degrees.

Many men had knocked upon the door of Estrella's

heart, but none had been allowed entrance. Although her suitors admired her talent, they also found themselves to be diminished by the bold enormity of it.

"In truth," she told me, "sometimes I shock even myself! When I am onstage I feel like a prize bull in the Plaza de Torros; powerful and yet trapped within the arena of my performance. Sometimes, I will catch the eye of a man on his own and will dance for him as though nobody else exists. As we lock eyes, an incredible feeling comes over me and I lower my head, imagining myself lifting him out of his seat with my horns. Just like a bull is how I feel! "

She took a long sip of her café con leche and sighed. "But of course what I really want is for that man to transform himself into a matador, so that when I lower my horns, he can leap to the side in his great suit of lights and wave his red cape, allowing me to pass through to the other side. You understand?"

I understood. It wasn't just any man Estrella desired, but one suited to her temperament; a partner in the whole dance of her life.

But such a man was slow in coming. The best her suitors could do, it seemed, was to hand her a single red rose as she left the dance floor, or to buy her a drink. After that, as soon as the romancing commenced, so too did their demands.

No man liked to share Estrella with the intense love of her fans, and one by one they asked her to abandon the stage for a quiet life of peaceful domesticity. It would never happen. Dance was not the best way for Estrella to live her life – it was the only way. Nothing else made sense. For her, the stage was a sacred place, where exposing her heart worked to set her free. She would be a traitor to her soul if she were to give up her art.

"What man would have me, and still let me do what I do? Tell me who that man is Gitana and I will go to him now. I will."

In my mind's eye, there flashed the image of Estrella's matador, waving his red cape, charming Estrella with his untroubled composure. The brilliance of Estrella's talent would stir him in such a way as to deepen his devotion. The intensity of her adoring fans, so many of them men, would not be a cause of anxiety for this brave matador!

Although I did not know the identity of this man, I had an idea for his character. I knocked upon the table three times, sending out a prayer for Estrella.

I knew her heart well – well enough to know with a certainty that one day he would appear. And on that day she would lay swift claim to his affections. Even the longest night will have an end.

Seeking the *duende*, there is neither map nor discipline. We only know it burns the blood like powdered glass, that it exhausts, rejects all the sweet geometry we understand, that it shatters styles.

The great Gypsy Flamenco artists of Southern Spain know that emotion is impossible without the arrival of the *duende*.

The *duende* works on the dancer's body like wind on sand. It changes a girl, by magic power, and at every instant works the arms with gestures that are mother to the dance of all the ages.

The *duende's* most impressive effects appear in the bullring.

The bull has its own orbit: the toreador his, and between orbit and orbit lies the point of danger... You can pass for a good bullfighter - but the *duende* is required to drive home the nail of artistic truth.

The matador who is bitten by the *duende* gives a lesson in Pythagorean music and makes us forget that he is constantly throwing his heart at the horns.

—Version of A.S. Kline's translation of Fredrico Garcia Lorca's *The Theory and Play of Duende.*

... All through Andalusia, from the rock of Jaén to the snail's-shell of Cadiz, people constantly talk about the 'duende' and recognise it wherever it appears with a fine instinct...

... I heard an old 'maestro' of the guitar say: "The duende surges up, inside, from the soles of the feet." Meaning, it's not a question of skill, but of a style that's truly alive; it's in the veins.

–Version of Tony Kline's translation of 'The Theory and Play of Duende' by Fredrico Garcia Lorca

Alejandro Sabicas

The whole of our street was buzzing with excitement: Sabicas himself had top billing at La Café de la Alegrìa!

Who is Sabicas? He is the finest flamenco guitarist in all of Spain; Gypsy royalty; a flamenco superstar!

Sabicas cut his baby teeth on the edges of his first guitar, and mastered it long before taking his first step. His guitar was the first thing he reached for in the morning, and the last thing he touched before closing his eyes to sleep. As a child, he had kissed it good night at bedtime and often slept with it, wrapping a protective leg over its curves.

How do I know all of this? I grew up with Sabicas. It was I who was responsible for keeping an eye on him while our mothers were away money making. During those times, young Sabicas and I adventured together. Our territory was all of Andalusia and we explored it fearlessly.

We fished from streams, picked wild berries, and explored the same mountain caves where bandoleers used to hide; all of those wonderful things the very young do, when left to their own devices. And wherever Sabicas went, so too did his guitar.

One time we ventured too far from the encampment. Many hours passed as we tried and failed to trace our steps home. We were hungry, very hungry, and so little Sabicas began to nibble upon the strings of his guitar, pretending they were Italian spaghetti.

Encouraged by my laughter he opened his mouth wide around the curves of the guitar, as though preparing to eat it in its entirety.

"Sabicas!" I mused, "If you ate your guitar, just imagine the terrible indigestion you would have."

He shot his finger into the air. "Indigestion," he announced, "in F minor!" And plucking away at the strings, he proceeded to coax hilarious belching sounds from out of his guitar.

"Excuse me!" He said, pressing his fist against his mouth, as though he too were belching. Then he raked at the guitar strings with his fingernails, causing it to whine miserably. "That," he informed me, "was the passing of wind!"

I waved a hand in front of my nose, "You don't say."

He rolled on the ground laughing; everything and anything could make him laugh, even his hunger!

Ah, Sabicas... He always rode in the back, feet dangling out of the caravan. The changing scenery of the passing countryside was a constant inspiration, and in the way of an artist, he transformed all that he saw into music. If his gaze fell upon the sheer drop of a steep mountain face, the steep edginess was reflected in his strum. Rough lanes and winding passages; the rocking to and fro of the caravan; sparkling water gushing through ravines, all of these things worked their way into his sounds. I traveled alongside Sabicas, watching what he watched and appreciating well his musical interpretations. A genius is what he was.

How was he now, I wondered. According to the pen and ink rendering of him on the poster advertising the night's performance, he was in possession still, of the same ear to ear grin. I looked forward to crossing his path at La Café de la Alegrìa! As there were a few extra posters at the news agents, I took one for the shop. Tonight would be a night to remember; however, we Spaniards begin our evenings long after the sun has set, and so there remained many hours of the day to work through first.

I entered the work shop and looked at the old clock upon the wall. It was almost time for a young lady by the name of Sundora to arrive.

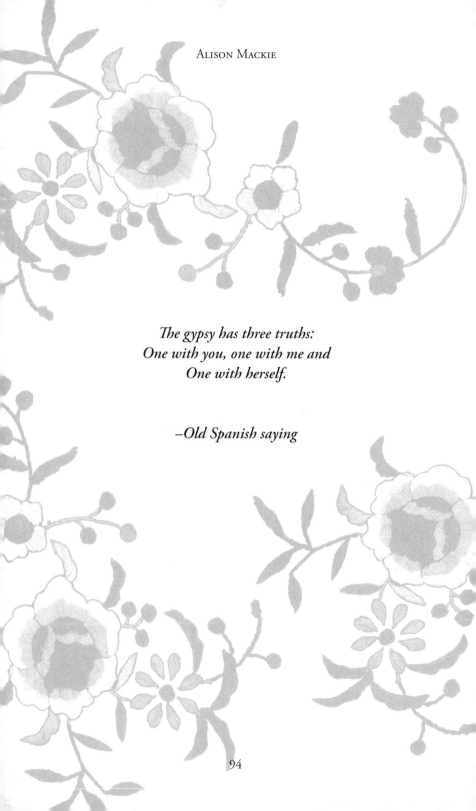

The gypsy has three truths:
One with you, one with me and
One with herself.

–Old Spanish saying

The Story of
Carlos and Sundora:
(A Fairly Typical Romance of Forbidden Love)

I was expecting the knock of a woman on her own-some lonesome. It was the first time in the history of our business that a woman had commissioned a Matrimonial Bed without her partner's knowledge.

The bed was to be a surprise wedding gift for her fiancé. Call me old fashioned, because that is what I am, but it seemed wrong somehow, in spite of these changing times, to invest in a Matrimonial Bed without one's partner. Something about the transaction did not ring true.

My hand was already upon the door knob, but I waited until she was finished knocking before opening the door.

Sundora's looks, though strikingly attractive, were difficult to place. Her radiant smile suggested an easy going confidence and so I took her to be a carefree young woman with a sunny disposition. However, just as a passing cloud will cast a shadow over the sunniest of climes, a sudden thought would completely darken her aspect, concealing her brightness. Such difficulty did I have in placing her ever changing aspect, that I could not determine whether she was strikingly beautiful or merely average; happy or sad. She was neither here, nor there. The image of a chameleon flashed through my mind's eye: Sundora was a master of disguise.

After exchanging a few pleasantries, she glanced over my shoulder in the direction of her Matrimonial Bed. The pupils in her eyes dilated, her hands fluttered to her heart, and in three easy strides she advanced upon the bed.

"The bed is just as I dreamed!"

So, I had a dreamer before me.

"Go ahead, lie down on your bed. Dream!" I waved my arm over the bed, which I had dressed in a sumptuous Paisley-patterned duvet. It was a lush looking space of jewel toned hues with matching drapery lined in gleaming silk and tied back at the posts with opulent golden ball tassels.

Sundora kicked off her shoes and made a flying leap onto the bed, every inch of her being filled with excitement. She picked up a fringed pillow and tossed it in the air. If she had jumped up and down on the mattress, I would not have been surprised. It happens; Tzigany's beds tend to enliven the spirit and summon up a child like joy. They are a soothing tonic, an energizing cocktail, a safe place in a crazy world. In short, they are heaven.

"So comfortable!" Sundora enthused, surprised.

This one was used to department store beds, I could tell.

"Goose feather mattress," I informed her, "Tzigany does things the old fashioned way."

"I love it!" She turned her body over, and then over again, luxuriating in the feel of her new bed.

A movement near the shop's entrance distracted me;

someone had quietly entered without knocking. I shot a scolding look, for the sign on the door made clear that knocking first was the rule.

The man at the receiving end of my dark look was Senor Carlos Castillos, a vintner whose face I knew well, as his parents, Juan and Alma, had been our very first customers when we settled in Ronda.

His dark eyes moved over Sundora with tender intimacy, and I realized at once he was her fiancé, so blatantly in love was his look. Profoundly involved with her new bed, Sundora was not yet aware of his presence in the room. He stood facing her, and his eyes deepened with longing as he watched her explore their bed.

Sundora moved her hand over the grooves carved into the headboard, tracing with her finger the turning curves of the heart. The magic is in the curves, not in the angles, Tzigany often says.

Carlos cleared his throat, startling her, and she turned in his direction. At once, she shot up and out of the bed. He nodded. For a brief moment, silence.

Carlos was first to speak. "This bed is very fine, Senora Torres."

Although he directed the comment to me, he stared at Sundora as one transfixed.

"My parents have one of your beds, as you know," he added, his voice thoughtful, soft. "Tzigany's gift is as strong as ever, I see."

"Thank you Carlos, I shall relay the compliment." I clapped my hands together. "So, with only two weeks till your wedding, this bed shall soon belong to the two of you!"

"I wish," Carlos remarked in a dry tone.

"I wish? What a curious thing to say!" said I, prompting an explanation.

"Not so curious when you consider that Carlos is not my fiancé." Sundora eyed Carlos. Her cheeks flushed and a lock of hair fell over her eye.

I looked from one to the other, and back again. "You mean to tell me that the two of you are not engaged to be married?"

Sundora cleared her throat. "I am in Ronda to buy this bed, and also to paint a portrait of Senor Castillos for the label of his new wine. I should have introduced the two of you, but you already seemed to know one another." She was flustered. "Forgive me Senora Torres, it is so close to my wedding date, and lately I don't know where my mind is at."

Maybe she did not know, but I did. I narrowed my eyes. "Are you quite sure you two are not getting married?" I asked politely. "Because, it seems fairly obvious something is going on here, and that the two of you are in fact well suited for one another." I crossed my arms.

Carlos flashed a long hot look at Sundora. I knew this look. He had seen her naked. I was sure of it.

Uncomfortable with the direction in which the conversation was headed, he bowed in my direction. "I have enjoyed our visit Senora Torres." Turning to Sundora, he added, "I'll be waiting for you across the street, at La Café de la Alegrìa." With that, he turned and left the shop.

Sundora collapsed onto the bed and groaned.

The young woman named Sundora was clearly in need of someone with whom she could speak freely. Untying the silken tassels at the bedposts, I closed the drapery of the bed, enclosing it completely, making it as safe and quiet as a confessional chamber. I lay down beside her, and reached for her hand. She squeezed it, and like women everywhere, I understood.

I spoke in a low tone. "The way Senor Castillos looked at you, I naturally assumed he was your fiancé."

She sighed.

"Sundora, I hope you do not mind my saying, but it would seem he has something going on for you."

"It would seem, yes."

"And your feelings for him?" I boldly enquired, although I knew the answer well: She too was in deep.

She looked away before answering, an indication that she was hiding the truth, perhaps even from herself. I awaited her response, wondering what kind of beautiful lies she was capable of telling. "You have to understand that Carlos and I met only yesterday! I'm not sure what I feel."

I looked at the engagement ring upon her finger. "Will you be changing your wedding plans?"

She was visibly displeased by my comment. "I can't cancel my engagement because a handsome stranger has walked into my life can I?"

"Can't you?" I raised my brow.

The suggestion took her by surprise; until that moment she had not even considered it a possibility. I plumped up a pillow and settled in by her side; we had a long talk ahead of us, Sundora and I.

Touched by my concern, she gave me the full reckoning.

Appointment in Ronda

Sundora held the photograph of a strikingly handsome man in her hand, and smiled to herself as she studied the details: Seated on a low rustic bench in front of a grape vine, the man in the photo had strong arms beneath his white linen shirt, with sleeves rolled up to the elbows. The late afternoon sun cast an amber glow upon his skin. To touch his gleaming black hair one would surely feel the heat of the sun.

Studying the photograph awakened her instinct; an excited buzz from within. She knew, because she had been told, that he was a wine maker of high repute. What she had not been told, but had sensed, was that he was the type of man who balances hard work with pleasure. There was something else tugging at the edges of her mind, and she smiled at the realization of what it was: This wine maker was an excellent lover; the type who had always been a faithful visitor to her dreams. She took in every detail, fascinated by the countenance of the handsome stranger.

"His name is Carlos Castillos," her mother said, pulling a weed from out of her garden. "And he has commissioned you to paint his portrait over the following week. The portrait you paint of him will appear on the label of his new wine."

Sundora shook her head. "I can't do it. I have a wedding to attend … my own, in case you've forgotten."

Ana clucked her tongue. "How could I forget your wedding Sundora? Did I not arrange it myself?" She smiled in the way that she did when she had the last word hiding beneath her tongue. "Tomorrow you are traveling to Ronda to purchase your Matrimonial Bed, is this not so?"

"It is so." Sundora shot her mother a sidelong glance; what did her trip to Ronda have to do with painting Senor Castillos?

Ana reached into the pocket of her apron and pulled out a map. "As it happens, the Castillos Wine Estate is just outside of Ronda. So, you can see to your bed in town, as well as paint the portrait. There is a guest cottage, but I won't be joining you. There is far too much work around here that needs doing."

Still, the whole thing would be rushed. Sundora usually required several weeks to complete a single portrait, but Ana had determined that this particular commission was far too important to turn down. There was not much time, it was true, but there was enough time, and so she accepted the Castillos commission on her daughter's behalf.

"The wine will be marketed internationally, which means your handiwork will appear on bottles all over the world! Your career will quickly advance Sundora."

Ana clapped her hands together with an air of finality, jangling her many bracelets. Dictatorial, she managed Sundora's career as well as her life. It had always been so. Ana was matron and boss; queen of the family tribe. In short, she was a force to be reckoned with. And reckon with her, Sundora always did, by doing exactly as she was told. But although Ana had control of Sundora's movements, she was completely unaware of the deeper activity taking place inside her daughter's mind.

Sundora was in possession of a great many thoughts about life which were directly opposed to those of her mother; thoughts she wisely kept to herself, for conflict with Ana, Sundora had learned early, was always a losing proposition, and besides, she liked to please. It made life easy. Whatever path her mother mapped out for her in life, was the path Sundora would follow.

Ana determined whom she would paint, just as she had chosen her future husband: A good Gypsy man, of course! To marry an outsider was unthinkable; if their people married whomever they pleased, their entire race would have disappeared centuries ago. With Gypsy blood on all four sides, the old ways ran deep; Ana's feet were planted firmly in the past. Tradition decrees that Gypsy girls are to be chaperoned by their mothers until such time as they are married. And when they do marry, their virginity is carefully inspected and usually found to be very much intact. Under her mother's eagle eye, Sundora was no exception.

If an outsider happened to overhear their conversation from the other side of the white garden wall, he would judge their family to be out of step with the modern world. And he would be right. Be that as it may, Ana understood well, that the ancient laws passed down from generation to generation served to preserve their culture and keep their blood pure.

Sundora watched her mother tread the rocky soil of her market garden. Her body moved with the tenseness that comes of vigilance. But fierce as her vigilance was, it was impossible to keep the garden free of weeds. Ana stooped over with her spade to dig out by the root a large dandelion. As she raised the plant from out of the ground, its delicate seed head burst in the wind, scattering in all directions, falling back into the soil. She shook her head with irritation and dropped her spade. She'd had enough weeding for one day.

Sundora transferred the pile of weeds to the burn pile at the far end of their plot. Taking a moment to stretch her tight muscles, Ana arched her back. Observing through narrowed eyes, she watched the way her daughter moved about the garden. Her girl was no longer a girl, but a woman; an alluring young woman with hips that swayed with her as she walked. By this time next year, Ana reckoned, she would be calling herself a grandmother. She clapped the soil out of her hands and led the way into the greenhouse, where the task of propagation awaited.

Sundora sliced a scion in bud and held it in place as her mother wound the grafting tape, joining the plant parts so that they could grow as one.

Most people assume that fruit trees grow from seed. This is not the case. If you grow a fruit tree from seed, the resulting tree will be a hybrid of two plants, and its fruit will vary in size. Grafting on the other hand, ensures that the new plant will be exactly like the plant from which it came.

Ana glanced warmly at her daughter as she wound the tape and Sundora smiled out of habit, over the saplings. She was not overjoyed with her mother's choice for her husband, but disobeying Ana's command meant being cast from the tribe. Marriage was by far preferable; a Gypsy without a tribe is no Gypsy at all.

Ana found the warm and humid atmosphere of the greenhouse to be deeply soothing. She loved the controlled environment. It was the only place she felt truly relaxed. Well, there were no weeds to pull, after all. She hated weeds. If only she could grow her daughter in a greenhouse, she mused, then she would not have to worry about seeds dropping where they do not belong; the cross pollination of cultures was a constant threat. Sundora's wedding was timely indeed. If she had waited any longer, the chances were slim that Ana could keep the bloodline pure for another generation. No question: Sundora was ripe. It is for very sound reasons that Gypsy girls are married off young.

Sundora took the photograph out of her apron pocket and placed it upon the work table. There was something about the wine maker's aspect that, as a bride to be, she sensed she would do well to avoid. His eyes communicated a rare promise; the type of promise to which she was highly receptive. With only a few weeks till her wedding, a wedding which represented freedom from Ana, if nothing else; it was the nature of this receptivity that put her on edge.

"You realize of course, that if I paint this man, I shall most certainly end up in bed with him," she remarked in a flat tone, as though joking.

Ana rolled her eyes, "You have obviously heard of his reputation as a playboy!"

Sundora had not heard, actually.

"Senor Castillos is said to enjoy making his fine wines just as much as he enjoys his second career: Making beautiful women." Ana snorted; this type of man did not impress her.

Nor did they impress Sundora.

"I trust you to take care of yourself in the presence of that one," Ana sniffed, straightening out the wrinkles of her shawl.

Sundora held the photograph a little closer, reassessing the wine maker's image. Strange. She never would have taken him for a playboy. Her skill in reading people, it seemed, was at an all time low.

"No worries, all will be well."

She needed to give her head a good shake. It had been foolish of her to read so much into a photograph. Pictures lie. And who should know better than she? Her paint brush had told more than its share of lies, certainly.

"Careful as you go!" Ana handed the well marked map to Sundora. A line drawn in red traced the route she would have to follow in order to reach her final destination. With her finger, she followed the winding path through the Serrania de Ronda mountains.

"Oh wonderful," Sundora deadpanned. "Just what every bride-to-be needs: A career playboy to take the edge off those last-minute jitters."

She had meant it as a joke, but it did not come off. Ana was not amused.

A Good Lover is ...

I listened carefully to Sundora's story, taking in every detail. Ana was a typical Gypsy mother whose type I knew well. Sundora rolled over to face me and I caught a whiff of Egyptian Musk. Strong and womanly, it was a scent she would soon grow into.

"You have to understand Gitana, in spite of my upbringing, I have very strong opinions on the matter of sexuality - my own opinions, not ones that my mother shares." There was a glint in her eyes, and her smile was playful. Sundora wanted to share those opinions with me.

"Go on," I said, raising a brow, and we entered into a spirited discussion about love and sex, a subject to which our Sundora warmed. I felt honored that she was sharing such intimacies with me, knowing she had been unable to do so with her mother.

"A good lover would be capable of making love to me using only his eyes."

Even in the photograph, Carlos's eyes had reached a part of her no man had ever touched.

"...A good lover would reach across the table and cover my hand with his, at just the right moment."

And apparently, Carlos's timing had been perfect.

"Sounds like the real thing to me." Said I.

Sundora wrenched her hands together. "It's probably just an infatuation. I need to know the truth."

"Sundora, there are lies more believable than the truth."

This gave her pause.

"I'm curious; tell me, what inspired you to buy one of

Tzigany's Matrimonial Beds?"

She shifted. "I've known my fiancé since childhood. I like him well enough, but sadly, there are no romantic feelings. *Nada*." The empty look she gave to me was full of meaning. "My greatest hope was that a charmed bed would transform my lack of interest into passion."

Since we cannot get what we like, let us like what we get.

I shook my head. "Tzigany's beds are indeed phenomenal, but without love, one is just going through the motions. Not good."

We spent the afternoon sprawled out upon her Matrimonial Bed, sorting through the intricacies of her love life. If Tzigany had happened to walk through the door, he would have known better than to stay. However, he was busy holding a meeting of his own at La Café de la Alegrìa, where he had crossed paths with none other than Senor Carlos Castillos.

Man to Man

Tzigany greeted Carlos Castillos with a nod as he entered the cafe. In response, Carlos waved him over to his table. Although he had only entered the café to settle his account, there was a sense of urgency to Carlos's invitation which Tzigany could not ignore and so he joined the young wine maker at his table.

Certain there was something more to Carlos's display of congeniality, Tzigany waited with interest to learn what that something might be. He did not have to wait long.

"What a coincidence it is to see you Senor Torres," Carlos said, pouring a glass of wine for him. "The woman I love is across the street buying one of your beds." He nodded in the direction of the workshop.

Tzigany raised his brow. "So, why aren't you with her?"

"Because I'm not marrying her." Carlos sipped from his wine. "Someone else got to her first."

Tzigany folded his arms and settled into his chair. "Tell me," he said.

And so Carlos recounted his tale, beginning with his first sighting of Sundora:

"The instant we met, her eyes claimed me, just like that!" He snapped his fingers. "You know?"

"I know." Tzigany nodded; he knew.

"After her eyes, I was a different animal. That was me, done. My search was over. She was the one. You understand?"

Tzigany understood.

In the space of a heartbeat, Carlos realized a profound interest in the dazzling artist who stood before him extending her hand in greeting. Her red silk skirt fluttered in the breeze, and he became aware of her intriguing scent; jasmine, moss and sandalwood. Her hands bore the stubborn residues of oil pigments: Alizarin crimson and Prussian blue. Carlos was smitten.

Sundora extended a hand in greeting, and impulsively, Carlos took both of her paint stained hands into his, and raised them to his lips. It was an old fashioned signal of interest which matched his intentions perfectly. His enthusiasm was short lived however, as his bottom lip snagged upon her diamond engagement ring. Surprised, he drew back quickly and cleared his throat. So, this beauty was engaged! The diamond sparkled in the bright sunlight between them.

"What happened next?" Tzigany asked.

Carlos shrugged. "I turned the conversation to the weather, naturally."

"Naturally," Tzigany nodded.

After a short discussion about the lack of rain, Carlos led Sundora toward the courtyard. There, beneath the shade of an ancient olive tree, they sat upon wicker chairs and made the requisite small talk. It was all business: Carlos mentioned suitable locations in the vineyard where the portrait might be painted, Sundora asked a few relevant questions, and they arranged to meet again later that evening, to tour the grounds. Formalities concluded, the time had come to show the artist to her guest cottage.

As Sundora rose from her chair, a sudden gust of wind made easy work of her skirt, lifting it high above her legs, exposing the curves of her hips, and more. Her long well-muscled thighs were tan, like *café con leche*, and a very pleasing contrast, Carlos observed appreciatively, to the provocative white triangle of her silken finery.

She blushed in embarrassment and Carlos raised his

shoulders high, shrugging expressively, as if to assure her that the whole thing was no big deal, really.

"This, of course, was not the case!" Carlos grinned.

"And every schoolboy knows it!" Tzigany said agreeably.

"A high voltage current shot through my body, as you can imagine."

"I can imagine," Tzigany imagined.

"I was deeply aroused," Carlos laughed. "There stood I with a potent erection leaning against my left trouser pocket. What if she happened to take notice of the sudden change in the cut of my trousers?"

Tzigany shook his head, chuckling.

So Carlos had shrugged and then, affecting a brisk professional manner, gestured for Sundora to walk ahead of him on the path which led to the cottage. Sinking his hands deep into his pockets, he sighed.

Amorous Breezes

At the cottage door, Carlos suggested that Sundora take some rest after her journey, and quickly left the scene. He would return for her later.

The same breeze that had scandalously raised her dress, welcomed Sundora into the cottage. Blowing in through the open windows, the gentle gusts raised the sheer white curtains in long slow rolling waves. The cottage breathed with life, and Sundora breathed along with it. The wholesome and invigorating atmosphere of the place awakened high spirits within her, making her feel alive in a way she had not experienced since childhood.

She stood in the center of the main room and did a slow turn. Every corner of the place was charmed. In the kitchen, dried herbs and copper pots hung from the ceiling. Upon the rustic kitchen table a ceramic bowl filled with bright red tomatoes filled the air with their ripe scent. And over the tomatoes, there hung a wrought iron chandelier of six elegantly tapered beeswax candles. Deep alcoves in the ancient walls served as storage spaces, and Sundora discovered in one of them, a collection of beautifully bound first editions by Frederico Garcia Lorca.

In the bedroom was a handsome bed constructed of a dark ancient wood that looked as though it had been around since the days of Columbus. Like the kitchen table, it too was rustic and carved only to soften the edges.

A blur of movement outside the window caught her eye, and she turned in its direction as a puffy white cloud hastened past at eye level, hurried along by the wind. Of course, she was in the mountains! Stepping out onto the balcony, she watched the cloud as it continued along its path, casting a shadow far below. Looking down, she observed that the cottage was nestled into a small plateau at the edge of the cliff and that it was a sheer drop to the vineyard below, where row upon row of grape vines spread out in all directions over the hilly land.

Inhaling the beauty of the atmosphere, she was feeling her environment, as well as seeing it. Outside the kitchen window, the leaves of the olive tree rustled against one another in the breeze and the muslin curtains continued to rise and fall, drawing out the afternoon in a long slow dance. Plucking a sprig of rosemary from the kitchen, she crushed it into her palms, releasing its warm extravagant scent.

Her spirits high, she danced upon the tips of her toes into the bathroom, and after treating herself to a cold shower, returned to the balcony to dry. She found the penetrating heat of the sun to be deeply soothing, and the little gusts of wind that kissed at her still damp body filled her with sensation. Relaxing into a lounge chair, she loosened the towel, exposing her skin to the elements.

Was there no end to the pleasures of the little cottage? Fetching a plump tomato from the kitchen, Sundora bit into it, and although she sank her teeth into the ripe flesh with great care, some of the insides gushed out, leaving a luminous trail of seed along her wrist. Like a cat, she cheerfully licked her skin clean, wondering idly if there was anything finer than the taste of a perfectly ripe tomato picked fresh from a garden. She thought not.

Her thoughts turned to the event in the courtyard. The wind had lifted her skirt high above her hips; an eye popping view for any man, it had to be said. She might as well have been naked! And yet Carlos had merely tilted his head to one side and squinted, as though observing a painting at the museum. In response to her embarrassment, he had raised his shoulders and offered to her, a simple shrug, as if to say: It's perfectly natural that your dress should fly up in the wind, just as it is perfectly natural that I appreciate the view. And he had appreciated the view, she knew well, for his attempt at concealing his appreciation had not been successful!

Sundora smiled, remembering his shrug. Playboy or not, she felt comfortable in his presence.

Drowsy with harmony, she dream-gazed at the passing clouds. The soft breeze continued to play over her bare skin and she entered into that state which feels like sleep, but is not yet sleep. In her mind's eye, the clouds floating past began to resemble other things. One cloud looked very much like a giant bottle of wine, Sundora mused, and just as her eye lids began to flutter, she caught sight of a cloud that assumed the unmistakable shape of Carlos's appreciation.

What if?

Sundora woke from her nap and dressed. Sitting down at the kitchen table, she noticed a press release peeking out from beneath the bowl of tomatoes:

At the tender age of fourteen, Carlos Castillos bottled his first wine for market. The wine was a great success. A bottle of champagne was poured over his head and Carlos Castillos was christened 'Spain's youngest wine maker' gaining notoriety in the wine making industry.

By age 17, Carlos Castillos took control of the family's old-fashioned winery, transforming it into a shining example of modernity. The intense extraction process Carlos introduced took as much from the grape as possible, resulting in a dense, flavorful broth. The wines he created were a hit with both wine critics and consumers alike, and demanded top prices. The Castillos Winery was making money hand over fist, but still, Carlos was not satisfied. To him, there was sameness to the style of these New World wines. As to their terroir - whether they were produced in Spain, Australia or California, it was impossible to tell, so alike were they in flavor.

Although these wines were pleasing to the international market, they were no longer pleasing to Carlos. He found that he favored complexity and subtlety over big fruit-driven wines. However, it is impossible to introduce fine layers of complexity to a dense wine, and so Carlos Castillos set himself a new goal: He would employ modern high tech methods, but this time with the intention of recapturing the glory of Old World wines.

From the beginning, Carlos's vision for 'Imprint' has been to create a classic; a wine both subtle and elegant that will improve with age. Carrying out his vision has been an act of defiance, for popular demand these days most decidedly favors New World styles of wine. For Carlos, the making of 'Imprint' has been an exciting gamble. But will this gamble pay off? Carlos Castillos thinks so, and graciously invites you to taste 'Imprint' to judge for yourself.

Three knocks sounded upon the door. Sundora returned the press release to its place beneath the bowl.

Opening the creaky cottage door to Carlos, the sudden force of his gaze nudged a second door inside of her. Her heart exploded inside her chest and she held his eye for as long as she could stand it before closing the door tightly behind them. As they made their way towards the vineyard she considered the magnetic properties of his gaze. His was the enchanting glance of a mesmerist and played tricks upon her heart, casting all manner of spells. If only she could paint his portrait without actually meeting with his gaze. Now there would be a trick worth learning.

In his turn, Carlos found it impossible not to stare; Sundora's cheeks were blushed with sun and her tousled hair fell loose and messy about her shoulders, as though she had just climbed out of bed. The thought of Sundora in bed gave him pause.

The evening air was dry and the large grape leaves waggled to and fro in the warm gusty breeze as they toured the vineyard.

Sundora had glimpsed within Carlos a clear and confident mind, completely untroubled by doubts. Surely though, he must have some worries to keep him awake at night. According to the article, he was bankrolling the future of his family's winery upon the release of an Old World wine. It was a high-risk venture. What if consumers did not respond favorably? What if he failed? What if the vineyard was plunged into bankruptcy? She was in awe of the utter boldness of his venture.

"I read the press release for Imprint."

"And?" He was interested in knowing her thoughts.

"And I am astonished by the risks you've taken! It made me wonder: Do you ever ask yourself *what if?* What if I've made a terrible mistake?"

"I never make mistakes." It was a bold statement to make, but one that happened to be true. "The grape is what I know, intimately."

A large grape leaf nodded in agreement by his head, tickling his ear, and he stepped to one side.

"To ask what if, is to allow fear to guide you through the unknown. Why would I want fear, when I have my instinct?" He plucked a grape from off the vine and popped it in his mouth. "Anyway, I'm sure things will turn out well."

"But how do you know for sure?"

"I don't." He threw back his head and laughed. "One never really knows for sure Sundora."

"So, you never ask, what if?"

"Never," he avowed, looking her straight in the eye, "I trust my instincts in all things, always."

He told her the unfortunate story of the high wire artist. "Making his way across the wire, the high-wire artist asked himself: What if I fall? His answer filled him with fear: If I fall, I will die! The high-wire artist looked down from his great height and his knees knocked together. Trembling, he began to second guess each of his steps. In second guessing his steps, he began to falter, and in faltering he misplaced a step and fell to his death."

"So his fear killed him, not the risk." Sundora acknowledged.

"Exactly. Fear kills the self, just as trusting the instinct strengthens it."

Carlos scanned the darkening sky. It was time to head back, time to taste his wine with the artist who would be capturing its essence, and his, in her painting.

Sundora's stomach rumbled loudly. This was noticed.

"I think my instinct is telling me something."

He laughed, "Let's prepare a feast!"

Love is being stupid together.
–Paul Valery

Candlelit Cottage

The cottage was dark, and so Sundora lingered near the door while Carlos saw to the lights.

He laughed, knocking into several chairs before finding his way into the kitchen. Opening the refrigerator door, he pointed at the small light bulb within, "There is only one light fixture in this cottage, and this is it."

He closed the refrigerator door, and everything went dark again. Lighting a match, he moved swiftly from candle to candle, lighting one after the other. There were candles everywhere and Carlos lit them all. Soon, the cottage was suffused in a honeyed glow and smelled wonderfully of beeswax.

The amber light lent a magical quality to the bowl of ripe tomatoes on the table and highlighted the knots of garlic and herbs hanging from the ceiling. It was like stepping into a still life, one painted by an old master.

Reaching into an alcove in the kitchen wall, Carlos pulled out a bottle of wine. "My masterpiece: Imprint."

The bottle had no label of course, because she had yet to create it.

Carlos removed the cork and poured a measure into her glass. Nosing the wine, Sundora recognized its unique character at once. She took the liquid into her mouth and swirled it around her palate, allowing the full flavors to emerge. Distinct, yet subtle, the flavors sidled up to her taste buds slowly, as though shy to reveal everything at once. First to present was *terroir*: Imprint was a wine of the sun and the earth; flinty, elemental and distinctly Spanish. Wrapped in a delicate veil of oak were layers of leather, spice, chocolate and tobacco, with a smooth finish that had just enough raspberry sweetness to lilt the palette.

Carlos's high tech winery had served him well, for with it, he had managed to produce an Old World masterpiece. She was in the presence of true genius; such wines do not create themselves.

"Your wine is outstanding; the most delicious broth I have ever tasted." Sundora enthused.

"Thank you," he held the bottle over her glass. "More?"

"Why not," she said, warming to the idea of passing the evening with an accomplished wine maker and savoring his fine wine. She took another sip, treasuring the taste in her mouth. Oh but it was good.

Carlos took some herbs into his hands and crumbled them into a bowl. It was time to prepare the feast.

Kitchen Tango

The kitchen was small, and so they had to step around and about one another as they worked. While Carlos chopped and diced, Sundora squeezed past him to inspect the fully laden refrigerator, gathering up tomatoes, marinated green beans, and thinly sliced purple onions for a salad. Slicing thin a generous portion of spit-roasted lamb, she placed it upon a platter the color of saffron, to which Carlos added a garnish of rosemary. Perfecto!

Finding a tin of anchovies, Sundora rolled them up with a toothpick, and dressed them simply with olive oil, popping one into her mouth. Golden waxy potatoes and red peppers sizzled on the stove in a mixture of olive oil and butter, and between them, they took turns at shaking the iron skillet. They maneuvered energetically around one another in the tight space, intent upon their various missions.

The music Carlos had chosen enlivened their steps, transforming their movements into an engaging kitchen tango. Carlos tossed the large carving knife expertly in the air when he was sure Sundora was watching and Sundora ground the pepper with an exaggerated flourish, raising an eyebrow in his direction.

They drank up goodly portions of wine as they cooked, and because her stomach was empty, the wine went straight to Sundora's head. As he refilled her glass, he stepped in close. Close, so that her cheek was warmed by his breath and she could feel the undercurrent of his manly heat, drawing her in deep and fast.

It was the kind of closeness that hastens a trembling ache for more. He reached for her, placing his hands upon her hips, and the tension inside her muscles dissolved. She closed her eyes. It seemed her body understood well the language of his touch; she was hip deep in the feel of him. And very soon she would be in over her head, she knew.

She opened her eyes. Inhaling sharply, she turned away from the pleasures of his touch. Careful as you go, her mother's voice echoed.

The mind is a terrible master, but a wonderful servant, however Sundora was no longer certain which part of her mind was in control. Was it master, or servant, who had just resisted the pull of her desire?

Carlos silently cursed himself. Sundora was interested in him he knew, but in the last analysis, she was engaged to be married. He would have to be more careful, he realized; careful so that his next attempt at closeness was met with success. He wanted to go to bed with this woman, engaged or not, but would get nowhere, if he moved too quickly. The moon, when reflected in water, slips through the hands. Carlos discerned within Sundora a longing for the element of earth; for solid ground, and with an instinct finely attuned to the moment, he worked toward grounding her mood.

The soft melody playing in the background had come to an end, and a bright bugle fanfare pierced the air. It was a lively *paso doble*; the music that summons the presence of a bullfighter into the ring, and so Carlos drew himself up into the masculine stance of a matador. Thrusting his hips forward and his shoulders back, he swaggered about the kitchen, waving a red linen tea towel in Sundora's direction.

Sundora laughed heartily, both delighted and relieved with the comical interlude. His playful attempt at impersonating a matador had diffused the sexual tension well.

"Me matador, you bull," he explained, pointing with his finger.

Whether it was his inspired playfulness or the wine talking, Sundora could not say, but she lowered her head, game. Giggling merrily she charged towards the red towel, completely caught up in the spirit of play.

"Bulls do not giggle, Sundora," Carlos reprimanded her sternly. "You are a very poor bull." He shook his head slowly, as if disappointed in her performance and Sundora sighed, happy, if not a little tipsy.

As the food was ready, they placed their fully laden plates upon the table and commenced to eat. The length of the table separated them only by a few feet, but the strength of his gaze made the distance feel even shorter. His glance was a physical thing and when she met with it, her entire body responded. A fire had been lit.

For dessert, she prepared espresso and poured it over cups filled with vanilla ice cream, tossing a few chocolate covered almonds over the top for good measure.

Relaxing into her chair, she noticed for the first time,

an old wine barrel in the corner of the room. In a childlike scrawl, the label affixed to its side, read: "Carlos's First Time Wine."

She gestured toward the barrel inquiringly. "First time wine?"

Carlos smiled. "I was six, maybe seven years old. It was harvest time, and I was ready to call myself a wine maker. So my father gave me a pile of grapes and set me loose. I stored my first wine in this barrel. And if I am not mistaken, there is still a little remaining inside."

Sundora found that she was not listening to his story so much as hanging on his every word. Soft, low, and full of gravel, his was a compellingly deep and manly voice. When he leaned back in his chair, she found herself leaning forward.

For his part, Carlos suppressed the urge to move closer. This time, he thought, I will wait until she is ready. I will.

As for Sundora, she was ready to go the distance. She was prepared to give up on tradition for the beautiful taste of his wine upon her lips, for his fascinating glance and for herself. She was done.

"What makes this wine so special?" Sundora nosed it thoughtfully, meeting with his eyes.

Carlos blinked. "Knowing the right time to harvest is vital. Waiting, sometimes, can make a good wine, even better."

The long look he gave her was full of meaning. Was he not waiting at this very moment, for her to become ready for him? The fullness of time, it seemed, was near at hand; soon the ripe fruit would be falling into his palm, he knew. He rose from his seat, tipped the old wine barrel onto its side and there followed a mellow sloshing sound.

Carlos refilled Sundora's glass and a comfortable silence grew between them. When tasting wine, there is always something in its character that cannot be measured, something that can only be perceived; providing one is sufficiently aware, or sensitive enough.

Sundora was by no means a wine expert, but inhaling the mysterious fragrance of the wine, she contemplated its complex and subtle layers; deciphering it in her own way: The wine was very much of the moment. And the moment was captured inside of the wine. The alchemy of time had drawn from the past, in order to produce the present moment. This wine knew the magnitude of time, she reckoned, and would in time, know more.

Sundora closed her eyes and her head spun, just a little. She drank, maybe a little more than she should have. But never mind. Her imagination was at play in the same way it was when standing before a blank canvas, limbering toward the creation of something new.

However, it was not a canvas, but Carlos before her. She felt the quickening of her creative energies, as they shifted from thought to action. If I had my brushes and paints set up, she thought, I would start work on his portrait. I would paint Carlos now. She smiled. Oh how she would paint him!

Something about her aspect had shifted, subtle, but there, and Carlos watched, careful not to miss a thing.

When she opened her eyes, she opened them to take him in deep, but found that he was already there. They gazed steadily upon one another without blinking. His look told her: I am waiting for you.

Sundora tipped the bottle of wine over her wrists and

presented them across the table to Carlos.

Harvest time.

At once he lunged across the table and fell upon her wine soaked wrists, drawing them to his lips and kissing delicately her pulse. Gently, she brought her hands back, this time splashing the wine behind her ear. Her laughter was soft and low, and her movements strong, and sexually fearless.

Carlos rose from his chair and opened his arms to her. She stepped into them. Holding back a curtain of her hair, he watched his old fashioned wine trickle down the length of her neck.

"You complement this wine perfectly," he told her, brushing his lips over her skin, and she swooned at the sound of his manly voice so close to her ear.

Then he kissed her, tongue deep and soft inside her tasty mouth. Nothing could prevent their coming together now.

Gently, Carlos passed a wine-soaked hand over her secret smile and the alcohol upon her most tender of feminine skin caused a thrilling charge of heat, deepening her own.

Their eyes met in a new place, and there passed between them a potent look of love.

Into her current deeply, Carlos was drawn, meeting with her hips as she leaned into the curve of the barrel. Sundora thrummed to the him of him; she, woman to his man. The oak barrel creaked with every rock, and the wine splashed merrily within; little waves echoing the fervored pace above.

And then, ocean came calling, rolling in, in wave-after-wave-over-together-pleasure. He surged to her silky heat, tightening; spilling deeply, his seed.

Three Truths

I sighed. "Sounds like the real thing to me."

But no.

"I had a lot to drink," she reminded me.

"Even so!"

"I'm not sure Gitana."

"Is there anything you are sure about?" Sundora wasn't even sure that the shadow attached to her body was her own. She had perfected the skill of overanalyzing.

"It was just a last minute fling," Sundora explained, trying to make sense of the beautiful love she had made with Carlos. "To change the course of my life just because of a sexual experience would be foolish!"

And more to the point, altering the course her mother had mapped out for her since birth, demanded a courage which Sundora did not yet possess; not to mention what she perceived as a reckless disregard for Gypsy tradition. How best to help her navigate the uncharted waters ahead? I wondered.

"Carlos will be the lover tucked neatly away in my past. Everyone has one of those."

"I never had one of those," I replied flatly.

"Well I have to make some sense out of this, don't I?"

"Do you? Some things can never be fully understood Sundora, and sometimes, it's better that way."

Sundora frowned.

"The feelings I have for Carlos are too new, they are not tested."

"And the feelings you have for your fiancé have been

tested?" It was crooked talk. "How can you say that with lips still swollen from Carlos's kisses?"

Sundora studied me. "You are very wise Gitana."

I shrugged. "She who lives well, preaches well."

"If only I'd met Carlos first."

"You've met him now," I offered by way of reason, "better late than never."

"True, but I can't hurt my fiancé."

"Is this a good reason to marry someone, so you do not hurt them?" Sundora's invincible loyalty to a man she had already betrayed surprised me. She was putting the cart before the boyfriend. I rolled my eyes.

She stared in silence at the top of the bed canopy.

"If I were to cancel the engagement now, my mother would sew me into a sack and throw me into the river!"

I chuckled and patted her hand. Melodrama was actually a very good sign: We were getting somewhere.

"What does your instinct tell you Sundora?"

"My instinct means nothing in this situation."

"Your instinct means everything in this situation, and what makes you doubt it?"

"Carlos's history with women makes me doubt it," she answered simply, repeating Ana's gossip. "At the end of the day, Carlos Castillos is what he is: A womanizing playboy."

"Ah yes, playboys. The woods are full of them … So, did you ask Carlos to explain his amorous adventures?"

The blank look upon her face informed me she had not.

I leveled my gaze into hers. "And you believe everything you are told Sundora?" I knew something more of Carlos's 'reputation' than she.

The reverse side also has a reverse side: Carlos was not a playboy! It was his brother Pablo who had an insatiable appetite for glamour models and movie stars. Evidently, Ana had gotten the wrong end of the stick. The parrot says what she knows but does not know what she says!

I opened my mouth to inform her of this, but quickly shut it: Reassuring Sundora that Carlos was a man of honor would make things far too easy for her. She needed to work it a little. Her instinct, that is.

Sundora had before her, a life altering decision to make, and far more than my reassuring words, she needed to trust

her instinct and allow it to guide her. Smooth seas do not make skillful sailors. The ship was hers alone to navigate. I was merely an agent of the deeper changes she needed to make, and was absolutely certain of her ability to chart a path of her own. For, in confiding in me, was she not already half way there?

Of course, I was trampling roughshod all over the well worn path Ana had trained Sundora toward since birth, but what of it? Sundora was no longer a girl, but a woman; she had proved that by being with Carlos.

The clock struck the hour. It was high time to shed some light on the truth! Wherever Ana was, I hoped she was no-where near.

I turned Sundora's hands over in mine, palms upward, and leaned over them to get a closer look.

"You read palms?"

Did I detect a note of interest, perhaps hope, in her voice?

"I do indeed."

"I shouldn't wonder," she smiled.

"But wonder you often do," I replied. The double head lines engraved into her palm indicated she was a deep thinker. But the lines were crossed with others.

"What else do you see?" Sundora asked, genuinely curious.

I turned her palms this way and that, before answering. "I see that you have three truths: One truth with one man and a second truth with another."

"I don't need a fortune teller to tell me that. You said that I had three truths, what about the third?"

I smiled; she was with me.

"The third truth has much darkness surrounding it Sundora," I lowered my voice. "It is the truth you have with your self."

She frowned. "Why is there darkness surrounding my truth?"

"Eh, because you haven't shed any light upon it," I said, matter of fact.

She stared at her palms, alarmed. "You are telling me I don't know my own truth."

"It's right here," I pointed to the center of her palm, "plain as the alphabet."

"Of all people, I should know my own truth!"

"Like the back of your hand, your own truth you should know." I affirmed.

It seemed that Sundora was finally getting it, and I was struck, as always, by the power of the palm to convey where all else fails.

She drew her hands away, but I was not yet finished. "To know your own truth Sundora, you must first illuminate it."

There was a change in her aspect at these words. For every child who is afraid of the dark, there is an adult who is afraid of the light. But the choice was clear: She could live a darkened existence, or she could face her own truth. She looked up.

"Tell me how to illuminate my truth Gitana, and I will do it."

"There is only one way Sundora: Fearlessly."

"Then fearless I will be."

Sundora closed her eyes and opened her mind. She was

a tourist traveling deep into the heart of her own darkness; a complicated maze of dead ends and false starts. The darkness of the maze was familiar and therefore reassuring, and yet she recognized it for what it was – a trap that existed solely to prevent her from knowing her own truth. It was absurd; she knew every twist in the winding passageway of her maze, but never once did she realize that its very construction was circular - it led nowhere!

This small truth empowered her to seek out more, and she stepped into the shadows, illuminating parts of herself that she had long been denying.

It was a kaleidoscopic journey; one truth turned upon the next, changing the meaning of the whole. She envisioned how stepping away from her arranged marriage would hasten banishment from her tribe; how she would be cut off from everyone she had ever loved, as though she had never existed. It was an unpleasant truth to face ... Was it any wonder her melancholy darkness had always provided a certain reassuring comfort?

She felt a sudden need for tradition, but let it go, realizing with jolting clarity the loss of self such tradition demanded. It was a sacrifice she was no longer willing to make. With this insight, the maze began to topple, and the shadows they cast fell with them. A clear well-lit path appeared in its place, leading straight to the heart of her matter.

The light of her truth emitted a rosy glow, warming the cheeks of her smile. In her secret heart of dreams she stood, fully illuminated. Giddy, she turned a brave face toward the future. She knew what she knew.

Sundora opened her eyes. The fearful uncertainty that

once darkened her aspect was no more. Her eyes shone; she was resplendent with truth.

My job was over. The rest of the road was hers to travel. Little by little, one goes far.

I made a little joke to send my new friend upon her way.

"A wise woman once told me that with one behind you cannot ride two horses."

Sundora grinned. "Unfortunately, choosing the right man is far more difficult than choosing the right horse!"

I shook my head. "No, no. Choosing the right man is just as easy as choosing the right horse. Perhaps even easier …"

"Go on."

"Imagine you have two horses before you from which to choose. One horse is black and the other horse is brown. Which horse is the right one for you?" I asked.

Sundora shrugged. "The black horse?"

"Wrong answer."

"The brown horse, then."

"Wrong again!" I sang merrily. "The right horse is the one that gives the best ride Sundora, and one must choose a man likewise." There is no worse joke than a true one. "Am I right? I am right. I know it!"

She laughed full on from her belly, and I joined in with her. Throwing her legs over the side of the bed, she parted the curtains.

"Have you ever had to choose between two men Gitana?"

"No, but I had a devil of a time choosing between two horses once."

We laughed some more, then sighed, and as she left, I handed her the advertisement for Sabicas's performance at La Café de la Alegrìa.

Across the road, Tzigany and Carlos were finishing their tapas, washing it down with a glass of red wine each.

Carlos drained his glass. "Engaged to be married or not, I want Sundora for myself!" He banged his fist on the table, sending the forks bouncing off the plates.

"Enough talk!" Tzigany scolded. "What are you going to do about it?"

"I am going to her now, and not a second later," Carlos announced. He stood up, quick and bold, and his chair fell behind him.

"*Vaya!* Go to her then, and go now, before it is too late."

Carlos broke into a wide smile. "I will see you here tonight my friend, and we shall raise a glass to my engagement!"

"But you have to ask her first!" Tzigany said, jerking his head in the direction of the door. "*Vaya!*"

The minute I heard my first love story,
I started looking for you, not knowing
How blind that was.

Lovers don't finally meet somewhere,
They're in each other all along.

—Coleman Barks; Rumi

Love Birds

Carlos stepped out of the café onto the hot sidewalk, and looked over the road. He had words for Sundora; bright beautiful words all lined up in a row, ready to deliver.

"The moment I heard my first love story I began my search for you. And now that I've found you, all I want to do is marry your dark eyes … "

Carlos turned to see Sundora standing beside the entrance of La Café de la Alegrìa. Had he heard correctly? Had Sundora just proposed marriage?

"Will you marry me?" It was she!

Sundora reached out for his hands and brought them to her lips, her eyes holding his. Her earnest display of love on the busy street undid him. All around, the world was in motion: Mothers pushed baby carriages and carried bags of groceries, a kiosk vendor sold the afternoon papers, and a street cleaner jabbed the sharp end of his stick at the bright shiny candy wrappers on the street.

"I want to go the distance with you Carlos," she whispered. "I want it all with you, children, old age, everything." She drew him close. "The first time I saw you, I felt something come alive inside of me, and now I know what that something is. It is Love."

She held both of his hands in hers, waiting.

"Yes I will marry you! Of course!" His voice caught in his throat, she had taken him so completely by surprise. "I was intending to ask you the same question myself!" He exhaled relief, giddy with joy.

It seemed that Carlos brought out the audaciousness in

Sundora. First the wine barrel, and now this: Asking for his hand in marriage. "My instinct guided me to ask you," she explained.

"I don't know about yours, but I trust what my instinct is telling me right now," he said pressing the full length of his body against hers. "I'm going to marry you all over the place Sundora."

"That is very fine Carlos. But please, no more wine barrels, if you don't mind. I'm still pulling out splinters!"

Sundora threw back her head and laughed and Carlos expanded at the beauty of her laughter. One kiss followed another. He was drunk on the feel of her lips, the sound of her laughter and the warmth of her body.

Tzigany opened the door of La Cafe de la Alegrìa and stepped onto the sidewalk. He took pause at the romantic sight of Carlos and Sundora locked in fond embrace in the middle of the wide bustling walkway, utterly oblivious to the busy street scene taking place around them. Crossing the street to his shop with a cheerful loping gait, he whistled a merry tune. It was a very fine day indeed!

A policeman guided rush hour traffic safely down the road, a school girl turned a cartwheel and a boy released a bright blue balloon into the atmosphere, watching dreamily as it drifted high into the sky. In the middle of it all, the two love birds kissed one another as though there were no tomorrow. Oh sweet love, is there anything finer?

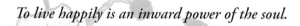

To live happily is an inward power of the soul.

—Aristotle

La Café de la Alegrìa

$\mathcal{L}$ater that night, Tzigany and I made our way through the crowded café, which at night transforms into a popular night spot; a cathedral of flamenco filled with fashionable society and flamenco aficionados. Vintage chandeliers sparkle with light, setting off the Moorish frieze in the ceiling above and the tile work below. One enters into the grand hall through several arching doorways. Upon a wall is mounted a festive sign, which reads: *A vivre que son dìas*, meaning: Live it up; life lasts just a couple of days.

The Alegrìa is a good luck café; one of those places where enemies turn into friends, everyone loves one another and lives get changed for the better. Translated into English, *Alegrìa* means jubilation, or happiness.

One drinks here to celebrate the fullness of life, not to eliminate emptiness. Families come together with friends, couples fall in love, and married couples rekindle their interest in one another. At La Café de la Alegrìa, anything can happen, and usually does.

I spotted my cousin Sabicas standing alone beside the

crowded bar. My heart leaped ahead of me as we crossed the room maneuvering around chatty knots of town folk nursing drinks and discussing world affairs; who is sleeping with whom.

Sabicas's mane of shiny black hair was shoulder length, his eyes sharp and intelligent. He had evolved from a skinny rascal into a strikingly sophisticated man. Upon his wrist he wore a Swiss watch and his jacket was clearly tailor made. He looked very much like what he was: A flamenco superstar.

His eyes lit up when he saw us. "Gitana!" He cried, grinning ear to ear in the way that he does. That man is a smile on legs.

"The very same!"

"The last time I saw you was at your wedding - five minutes after you met this gentleman here." He turned his smile towards Tzigany.

"A mistake I shall regret for the rest of my days," I grumbled merrily. In keeping with Spanish superstition, I was protecting what I had by underrating its value. In truth, our love had deepened perfectly over the years, and was so beautiful a thing that I could cry just thinking about it. But that is flour from a different sack.

"What about you Sabicas? Married yet?" Tzigany asked with genuine interest.

"Not yet, no." The room was filled with attractive women; many of them ready to test their charms upon Sabicas, we knew. A femme fatale sauntered past, ravishing him with her eyes. "I could be wrong, but I think I am ready for a change," he said, eyes downcast.

Tzigany puffed at his cigar thoughtfully, "No shortage of

female admirers."

Sabicas shrugged his shoulders. "All they want is to be wined and dined, and."

"*And?*" Tzigany tilted his head inquiringly.

"Yes… *and.*" Sabicas leaned on the word with meaning.

"Oh! *And!*" Tzigany laughed. "I see!"

And see he did, as yet another senorita stepped before Sabicas. This particular one I recognized as La Chicarona, a well known and dazzling firefly of the Seville night scene whose face I recognized from the newspaper gossip columns. It was reported that she was an actress of considerable talent who was featured in more than a few soft porn movies. And tonight it seemed La Chicarona was fly to some play, for when Sabicas stepped aside to allow her to pass, she matched his step, so that they remained facing one another. Her bedroom eyes flashed a clear invitation to which he responded by stepping in the other direction, but again she matched his step perfectly. I was delighted by the inventiveness of her bold courtship dance.

Sabicas, however, was not so easily impressed. He reached into his jacket pocket and produced a red carnation. Tucking it behind La Chicarona's ear, he told her that it had been his pleasure to meet her and sent her on her way.

Tzigany turned his head, observing how every man turned to watch La Chicarona as she strolled past. "She seemed a nice little package …"

"Tightly wrapped too," I added.

"But very loosely tied," Sabicas pointed out.

When looking for a wife, a Gypsy man is usually after

chastity.

"Anyway, there was no chemistry, and I don't care to waste time – hers, or mine."

"Water you should not drink, let it flow..." Tzigany intoned.

Sabicas took Tzigany aside to show him the workmanship that went into the making of his guitar, and I joined Juan and Alma Castillos at the bar. As usual they were surrounded by good cheer and jovial laughter.

Juan and Alma are an old but vibrant couple who married late in life. They were our first customers in Ronda. Carlos and Pablo, were born nine months later.

Time flies. To look at them one would never guess them to be nearing seventy years of age, for although their hair is silver and the lines on their faces deeply engraved from years of tending to their vineyard under the blazing sun, their eyes are clear and bright and radiate extreme good health. They are energetic and their supple bodies move with the quick and easy grace of athletes.

Several workers from their vineyard listened with interest as Juan entertained them with a humorous anecdote.

"Tell us another," they crowed to general mirth when he had finished his tale.

"No more stories, please!" Alma insisted. "I've heard them all a hundred times over. I say No to more stories, but Yes to more wine!" She raised her empty glass in the air.

Juan held the wine bottle up to the light, squinting theatrically. "The wine bottle is empty my dear Alma."

Alma affected a stubborn pose and held her glass out before her, resolute, waiting calmly for Juan to fill it. Juan turned the empty bottle upside down above her glass, and of course, not a drop came out; the bottle was indeed empty.

Instead of withdrawing her glass, Alma raised it even higher, so that it met with the long neck of the bottle and Juan countered this action by pressing the bottleneck down, inserting it ever deeper, right to the bottom of her empty glass, rotating the tip of it gently whilst raising a wicked brow over his shoulder. His antics summoned full bodied laughter all around.

Old Elvira Vega stepped into the circle. "Juan, I see you are in top form tonight," she said by way of greeting.

"Ah well, Alma has me on a diet …"

"Do you think that's a good idea at your age?" Elvira asked, winking at Alma.

Juan shrugged expressively. "She says it is healthier."

"But you've done alright up till now. If you change now, you will throw your body out of whack, get sick and die!"

"Yes, I think she is trying to kill me."

Alma slid her arm around Juan's waist and he kissed the top of her head.

Just then, Carlos appeared with Sundora and they stepped into the circle.

"Allow me to introduce Sundora. She is the artist who is painting my portrait for the wine label."

"Sundora, you are beautiful!" Juan gushed, bringing a hand to his heart.

"Don't mind him Sundora," Alma remarked with a laugh, "Juan is one of those people who becomes euphoric with one glass of wine."

Juan turned to allow space for a newcomer. "Oh look

who it is," he said, "Sundora, allow me to introduce Carlos's brother, Pablo. Pablo, this is Sundora. She's an artist!"

Sundora startled in Pablo's direction, unaware that Carlos had a brother.

For all of the physical similarities, Carlos and Pablo could not have been less alike. Pablo dressed in a flashy way and smelled of Paco Raban. His dark eyes bore into her with great intensity. Taking into account the devious charm and scorching heat of his gaze, Sundora realized at once the true origin of Ana's rumors: It was not Carlos, but Pablo, who was the womanizing playboy! Sundora shot a sly knowing look my way, which I returned with an equally knowing wink.

Juan clapped his hands together. "So Sundora, which of my sons are you interested in? Carlos or Pablo?"

"Neither, she's wearing an engagement ring!" Alma pointed out. "Men. They never notice these things."

"Engaged, are you? Who against?" Juan asked.

"Against Carlos," Carlos replied, drawing Sundora close. They exchanged happy looks and Sundora's diamond ring sparkled beneath the vintage chandeliers. They had obviously spent the afternoon at the jewelry boutique on the Calle Nuevo.

"I was not even aware you were seeing anyone!" Alma complained happily.

"That's because we met for the first time only yesterday." Carlos explained.

Juan nodded approval. "Love is like wine. When you find the right one, you just know."

"That's right," Alma affirmed. "Anyone who says love at first sight did not work for them, did not work at their love!"

Pablo turned to Carlos and Carlos to his father, and there was much back slapping and congratulations all around. Alma rushed forward to welcome her future daughter-in-law into the family with a maternal hug. Over Alma's shoulder, Sundora's eyes twinkled, and I touched my heart.

"You could have told me," Sundora cheerfully scolded, as she stepped out of Alma's arms.

"Told you what?" I smiled sly.

"You know what!" She jerked her thumb in the direction of the real playboy.

"Oh that," I remarked, looking at Pablo, "Finding out this way was far more interesting, don't you agree?"

Sundora squeezed my hand and like women everywhere, we knew.

Tzigany and I bought a bottle of cava to toast the newly-weds and Sabicas arranged for tables and chairs to be set out beside the stage for our merry gang. The place was heaving with people but somehow we managed to find space.

"So how are Raguel and Angicaro doing these days?" Alma asked when we were settled into our seats.

"They are in Africa, doing missionary work," I replied.

"Missionary work?" Juan asked, "What do missionaries do exactly? Do they promote missionary sex?"

Alma checked him in the side with her elbow.

Carlos edged his chair closer to Sundora while Pablo kept in constant eye contact with La Chicarona, who still wore the red carnation behind her ear.

A well known patron of the arts approached our table. Snobby, rich and overly aware of her place in society, she ignored the rest of us, addressing Sabicas only.

"Senor Sabicas, what would be your fee to play at my party?"

"Two thousand Euros," he replied, reaching for the cigar which Tzigany handed to him.

Her eyes widened. "Your fee is very high, but I will pay it," she said. "But please remember, you are not to mingle with the guests!"

"You do not wish for me to mingle with your guests?" He raised a brow.

"That is my wish, yes."

"I see. In that case my fee is reduced by half." Sabicas said without looking up. He turned to Tzigany, who held out a flame, and Sabicas proceeded to light his cigar. He did not feel like talking to the society lady anymore. Feeling the sting of his rebuff, she shot a worried glance at our table but there was nothing left for her to do but walk away.

"Please remember, you are not to mingle with the guests!" Juan mimicked the society lady after she was out of hearing range, and we all broke into delighted laughter. Gypsies are still held in very low regard by the general population; however Sabicas had turned the table on her well. Now that he was rich and famous, he could afford a little attitude on special occasions.

On nights like these, before the main act, the locals take turns performing for one another and so it went that Elvira Vega mounted the stage to announce the first act.

She had let down her long braids for the evening, and her hair, white as moonlight, glowed like a halo under the stage lights, brightening her face. She tapped lightly at the microphone just as handsome old Senor Perez appeared beneath the stage. Broad shouldered and wearing red pants, he leaned heavily on his cane, as he hastened past. Elvira turned in his direction and placed a hand upon her hip.

"Aaaah," she sighed, "if only I were seventy five years old again." The crowd responded with delighted laughter and Elvira winked mischievously.

She surveyed the crowd, most of whom were half her age and younger. "And while we are on the subject of age, why is it that everybody worries about getting old?" She shook her head, as though vexed. "I always tell people, I tell them: I never meant to get old, it just happened! And with luck, one day it might happen to you too!" Her salty comments sprinkled the room with laughter. Elvira knew well how to work the crowd.

Senor Perez shook his cane at her and she gave him one of her direct looks. "What did I do?" she asked.

"I look at you and I see trouble!" he cackled.

"Life is trouble! Only death is not!" Elvira shot back, quoting Zorba the Greek. "To be alive, you have to loosen your belt and look for trouble!"

The audience cheered in agreement.

"Ayieeee! Who will be first to perform tonight?" She cried out. "Will it be La Chicarona, sitting so pretty over there?" She pointed with her fan and there followed whistles and hoots of excitement.

"Or shall we begin with Elvirrrra Vegaaaaaa?" Elvira

crooned, drawing out the sounds of her own name with relish, and naturally everyone cheered encouragement.

"Very well, I shall be first to perform! But I must warn you that I have a very serious physical impediment which prevents me from performing normal everyday movements. It is called being ninety years old!"

"But Elvira," somebody called out cheerfully, "it's a well known fact that you are over a hundred!"

"Is that story still going around!?" Elvira enjoyed lying about her age. "I suppose it could be so; the older I get, the more I remember things which never happened, but it's pretty well established that I did get born!"

The audience scratched their heads over that one, and Elvira seized the moment, taking them by surprise: Her hands met over her head with great force, transforming her single hand clap into a crack of thunder. Striking her right foot hard and fast upon the stage floor she flashed the length of her arms outward, extending long bony fingers like bolts of lightning over the crowd. And just as it requires only a short space of time for lightning to strike, Elvira had managed to create a sensation with her brief performance. Excited applause abounded.

Taking up the microphone, she announced the next performer.

"Let us now welcome to our stage La Chicaronaaaa!"

La Chicarona bounded up to the stage and Elvira beckoned her towards the microphone.

"Chicarona, I understand you are visiting us from Seville, do you plan to stay in Ronda for good?"

"I am visiting here yes, but not for good." She said,

winking suggestively at Pablo.

"I seeeeeee!" Elvira raised a brow and continued. "So tell us Chicarona, do any of our fine townsmen in attendance this evening tempt you?"

"I generally avoid temptation," Chicarona replied, then added, "unless I can't resist it." Her smile was broad and her eyes sparkled with mischief. Elvira bowed, and left the stage.

I kept an eye out for Estrella de la Flamenca, the only one of our gang not present. It seemed she would be late this night.

Upon the stage La Chicarona was well into her performance. Her chief attraction seemed to be the daring way in which she showcased her breasts as she danced. Being the center of attention must have caused her some excitement, for her tetilas were at full salute; rock hard they strained like little pebbles against the sheer fabric of her dress. Her long brightly colored nails, stiletto heels and revealing costume brought to mind those glamour models who grace the covers of magazines, you know the sort I mean: The ones which horny men purchase to bring themselves to pleasure. La Chicarona was dressed to thrill.

In no way could she be considered a true flamenco artist; clearly her performance was intended only to fire the imaginations of men, and by her sexed up moves there was little doubt she had been in more laps than a napkin. Even so, her appeal paled in comparison to that of Estrella de la Flamenca. La Chicarona spat raw sex at the audience, whereas Estrella tapped into, and transmitted a sensibility all her own. Apart from Pablo the playboy, whose eyes followed Chicarona's every move, the rest of our table were far more interested in the talk of the day. Sabicas and Tzigany discussed the latest bullfights, while Carlos whispered tender sentiments into Sundora's ear.

Alma turned to Elvira, "What do you think of the way young women expose themselves these days?"

Elvira Vega shot a sidelong glance at La Chicarona. "Not much."

You have to understand that Alma, never having had any daughters of her own, felt a strong maternal streak toward young women such as La Chicarona. Alma shook her head. "I suppose it's better to be looked over, than to be overlooked," she conceded, "but whether the quality of attention Chicarona gains from such attention seeking behavior has any lasting value is a point she would do well to consider. The longer she engages in that way of life, the harder it will be for her to find true happiness." She turned to face me. "And you Gitana?" She topped up my glass.

"Ah well, when women go wrong, men go right after them." The cava bubbles tickled my nose as I sipped. "It used to be the only women who dressed and acted like that in public, were prostitutes. But look around…That dress Chicarona is wearing? It's called *porno-chic* and what's more, it's considered fashionable!" I shrugged, as if to say, what can you do?

"Porno-chic…" Alma tried the word out for herself and frowned. "Where do you pick up this lingo?"

I winked. Gypsies pick up language the way a mirror picks up images.

On stage, La Chicarona slid her hands over and around

the ample curves of her body, imitating the sensual move-ments of a woman taking a shower. Her hands moved with a deliberate slow grace as though spreading soapy lather over nakedness; as though she were thrumming to the feel of her own touch, which in fact, she probably was. Pablo's eyes wid-ened and he shifted in his seat.

"I have a theory that men who overindulge in porno are the world's worst lovers," I said, sipping the cava.

"I for one never look at those magazines!" Juan asserted with an exaggerated virtue that suggested otherwise. Elvira, Alma and I shot him a look.

"Well, maybe once or twice, but just a peek!" he said grinning.

"But a peek now and again is perfectly natural! What could be more interesting than naked bodies all tangled up in one another's arms?" I asked.

"And bent over too!" Juan added with enthusiasm.

Alma clucked her tongue sharply. Although she knew well that Juan did not partake of porno, and that he was only acting it up for the greater amusement of the table, she found his humor veering toward bad taste. It annoyed her, and so she quietly checked him under the table with a kick.

Elvira Vega leaned forward. "Your porno theory inter-ests me Gitana. How do you reckon men who buy porn to be bad lovers?" Her keen interest surprised me. Was she not over a century old, and therefore too ancient to be interested in such topics of conversation?

"Well, it's a purely intuitive theory, not drawn from ex-perience, of course!"

"Of course," she concurred.

"But it stands to reason: When a man looks at porno, his pene jumps up to attention just like that," I snapped my fingers, "but at what cost? Little does the porn addict know that that with every turn of the page, he cripples and deforms the muscularity of his own imagination. His natural ability to flex love to excess, to excite his woman in fresh and inventive ways, disappears! Porno has hijacked his imagination." The cava had loosened my tongue, I was on a roll.

"Close your eyes and picture this sad scenario," I instructed, and Elvira, Alma and Juan closed their eyes.

I began: "Imagine a woman and her husband are having sex. The husband is driving into his wife in his usual meaningless way."

"They are in their bed?" Alma wanted to know.

"Yes, they are in their bed."

"And they are completely naked?" Juan asked, "Or is his lady wife wearing some sort of ... silky clothing?"

Elvira rolled her eyes.

"Eh, they are completely naked. Anyway, the husband, who is supposed to be making love to his wife, is actually fantasizing about a porno model he saw on the pages of a magazine."

"And what does the porno model look like?" Elvira cracked wise.

Juan and Alma burst out laughing.

"She has balloon-like breasts and a blonde *pudenda*. Her lips are glossy pink and she rolls her tongue, as though there are cake crumbs at the edges of her mouth for which she is hungry."

Eyes still closed, the trio imagined the scenario, chuckling. Alma stabbed at the side of her mouth with her tongue.

"Anyway, Senor Husband's eyes are closed and the porno model, whom he has never before met, has pride of place, center stage inside his fantasy as he pounds away mechanically into his wife, and then, just as he is about to climax, he opens his eyes and catches his wife yawning and checking the time on her watch, and he wonders, why?! Why is his wife so bored, when he is on fire!"

Elvira slapped the table hard. "Why indeed!"

"She is bored because there is no connection between them. If she has become overly familiar with every little crack in the ceiling above the bed, it is only because her husband no longer has the ability to make love! There is a word for what he is doing to her - and it is not called making love."

"What makes a man a good lover then?" Again, Elvira's keen interest surprised me.

I thought about it. Where to begin? "It's all in the hands," I said, waving my fingers over my empty glass of cava, which Alma was quick to refill.

This time it was Juan who leaned forward, "It's all in the hands?" He raised a brow.

"Absolutely. If a man has a lot of heat inside his love, a woman can actually feel it in his touch. And when he mindfully fuses his heat with his love, his woman will rise to his occasion, every time." Whatsoever the mind can conceive, the hands can achieve.

Juan turned to Alma. "Is this so?"

"It is so."

Under the table he placed a hand on her knee, "What is

in my mind Alma?"

He did something with the pressure of his hand upon her knee, concentrating the heat of his love through his fingertips. She gave to him a Mona Lisa smile, transmitting back a message all her own. Their bodies shared a quiet understanding; nothing so obvious as words could tell the story of their love.

Out loud was for little jokes, laughter. Inside, all was quiet understanding. His arms enfolded her; she was a love letter inside the envelope of his embrace, yet to be opened. To they who understand, few words are needed.

Elvira raised a delighted brow, "It would seem these two are still capable of rattling the bedposts."

"Perhaps the charmed bed which Tzigany made for them all those years ago had a particularly potent charm," I ventured.

Elvira shot me a skeptical look. "Making love in a charmed bed may feel like magic," she said, "but magic is just an illusion. The true power of Tzigany's charm resides within one's imagination," she avowed, tapping at her skull. "If Tzigany's charm works, it is only because they believe in it."

I took Elvira's point, but agreed with it only half way, the other half of the equation was in fact due to Tzigany's supernatural gift. One has only to look at one of his beds to know that something is going on there, something that can not be easily explained.

"Elvira, for a mystic you are very skeptical!" Alma said, "Tzigany's beds are phenomenal. Sleep in one, and you too will know."

Elvira snorted. "I'd have to find myself a husband first; easier said than done at my age."

Elvira's broad shouldered friend leaned casually upon his cane behind her chair.

"And what are your thoughts Senor Perez?" Juan asked.

Without hesitation Senor Perez replied, "Women are born to love. They are born to fall in love, to be loved," and he bowed, tipping his hat at Elvira, "and to make love."

To our great surprise, Elvira blushed.

"Is that what you think?" She asked, her cheeks tinting a lovely shade of pink.

Elvira winked at me, her old eyes bright and merry.

"We'll have a drink later, you and I," she said, addressing Senor Perez.

"That would be very fine," her suitor replied with a bow.

As Senor Perez returned to his table, Elvira whispered into my ear, "Such a fine cut of meat, and I with no teeth!"

She opened her fan, pleased with the evening's turn of events. Evidently there remained some embers in her fire; embers which Senor Perez had well-stoked, transmitting memories of heat from long ago. Elvira fanned the glowing embers of her ancient hearth, taking great comfort in its warmth.

The atmosphere was charged.

La Chicarona took a bow in Pablo's direction. Inside the look she gave to him was a promise of hot and dirty sex; it was the kind of promise to which Pablo was highly receptive. Taking careful aim, she tossed the red carnation from behind her ear towards him, and it landed neatly in his lap. He gave her the nod. The lewd gaze she turned upon the crowd seemed to say, *come on boys, you know you like it.* But clearly, it was Pablo who would be getting it tonight.

Elvira rolled her eyes, closed her fan, and leaped out of her seat, clattering merrily up to the stage to announce the next performer.

And so the evening progressed. One after another various performers took the stage, until there remained the final act.

The sounds of laughter subsided, calls for more wine silenced and dominoes swept to one side as Elvira Vega welcomed Sabicas to the stage.

Sabicas, dressed all in black, looked immaculate under the stage lights. He acknowledged his audience with a friendly nod and sitting down, lowered the microphone until it was level with the sound hole of his guitar.

Turning his attention to his instrument, he did a warming up exercise in G major, a happy sounding chord which brought to mind the eating of juicy peaches.

As he tuned his guitar, he worked also at tuning the contents of his mind, integrating the tenor of his spirit with the spirit of his strum, deepening himself for the performance.

Sabicas summoned the notes at play, fitting them into structure, creating musical tension. Within the randomness of single notes, a pattern was emerging. Faster and ever more circular, single notes linked with chords; chords with rhythm; and rhythm in its turn, with melody.

The accumulation of notes seemed to suggest he was ready and all that remained was about to happen. He concluded his warm up and looked up at the audience.

Something Other

The hard driving rhythm of Alejandro Sabicas's guitar had only begun, followed by the usual shouts of encouragement, when a sudden disturbance distracted the crowd's attention from the stage. It was a latecomer, but not just any latecomer, for this was Estrella de la Flamenca, and the crowd shifted in their seats as one, turning in her direction, whispering "Estrella!" or reaching out to touch her as she passed their table. She shushed at them in turn, willing them to silence. But she was a star, and these, her most loyal fans in all of Spain, and so passing by without incident was not possible.

Sabicas released his guitar, squinting under the bright stage lights in the direction of Estrella's shadowy figure. An embarrassing silence filled the air and he tapped lightly upon the body of his guitar, waiting for the mysterious stranger to find her seat so that he could resume his performance. As he waited, a little smile played at the corner of his lips; his performance had been suspended in thin air, but apparently Sabicas was still enjoying himself.

I raised my arm to alert Estrella to my presence, which

she acknowledged with a little nod. Deeply embarrassed, she allowed a few seconds to pass before approaching our table.

Although Sabicas could not see Estrella, he was attuned to the pitter patter of her very fine step; like cloven hooves they sounded out, beating a path across the tiled floor of the café. Clip, clop, clip. At once, he picked up his guitar, and strummed right into the staccato beat of her footsteps, picking up on the rhythm of her stride in a teasing and light-hearted manner.

Taken aback by the unexpected accompaniment, Estrella stopped in her tracks and sucked in her breath. The crowd tittered, somewhat amused, for when Estrella's footsteps fell silent, so too did Sabicas's strumming. Estrella was vexed! She knew well that the instant she moved forward, Sabicas would take up where he had left off, making sport of her progression. Nevertheless, she set out once again, this time however, adopting a reserved, more formal stride; a pace both haughty and defiant. Clop … clop … clop.

On stage, Sabicas tilted his head and squinted theatrically; to his ear her new composition of steps resounded with uppity airs and graces, and he quickly deflated their pomposity with a *chuflas*; a carefree style that emphasizes spontaneity and humor. But if Sabicas was amusing himself, Estrella was most assuredly not, and wished only to put a quick end to his nonsense.

Rearranging her steps once again, she broke into a run. Clipppity, clip, clip. But there was no escape, for Sabicas's guitar followed quick upon her heels. Finding her seat at last, she fell into it with great relief, exhaling sharply.

A riot of laughter filled the air, and Estrella's cheeks

flushed with heat. She was not amused. Although not on stage, she had most certainly played a part in Senor Sabicas's little performance, and furthermore had been made to feel awkward before a crowd; a sensation she had never before experienced. Mutinous thoughts were quickly taking shape inside of her mind. Estrella was seeing red.

As the crowd settled, Estrella's outrage grew. She would not be played with. No she would not. She rose from her seat, and lifting her long flamenco skirt, slowly climbed the steps to the stage, allowing each step to fall with an exaggerated clomp. The crowd was with her. Everyone leaned forward in their seats. Magic was afoot. The air crackled with electricity. Estrella was on fire, we knew, for we knew her heart well.

It is better to arrive at just the right moment than to be invited. Estrella advanced upon Sabicas, cool, walking it out slowly from her hips; her footsteps much louder than necessary. And just as he had made light of the sound of her step with his strum, her pacing now served to intensify its absence; the silence between each step created tension, suspense.

She turned to face him, flashing him a look of fiery sentiment, and landed her right foot upon the floor, drawing herself up into a graceful flamenco pose. Her skirt fell open at the thigh, exposing the long muscles of her leg against red silk lining. And all was still, except for the slow tensing of her calf muscle. Nobody could do more with a flexed calf than Estrella, she was unreal!

The great stillness of her pose was a calm before the storm. Electrified, our hair stood on end and we held our breaths in anticipation. The storm, we knew, was about to break.

At once, she raised her skirt, and brought down from

the sky a hailstorm of sound, as her feet battered into the stage a raging zapateados; a rhythmic combination of steps and sounds using the toe, sole and heel of the foot. Under the force of her strenuous exertions the stage floor trembled and Sabicas felt her vibrations rise up and into him through the soles of his feet, rousing the magical force known as duende. The barrage of sound filled him with sensation; the woman before him was a force of nature.

Finishing her footwork, Estrella placed her hands artfully upon her hips, and drew herself up at the chest. Make something of *those* foot steps, her haughty bearing seemed to say.

Sabicas was deeply stirred. He leaned into his chair, enthralled by Estrella de la Flamenca. That was him, done. After her footsteps banging away in front of him like that, he was a different animal. There was no going back.

When the mind races so too does the heart. His red deep-fibered world had expanded to the rhythm of Estrella's footwork, for she had kept perfect time with the accelerating beat of his heart, and in doing so, made an impression upon his soul. His blood surged from his root to his height and back again.

No man shows his soul to another man, he shows it only to a woman. But we all bore witness as Alejandro Sabicas offered his soul to Estrella.

Estrella felt a spark of understanding shoot up between them and fall upon the kindling of her soul, setting off a blaze of warmth; creating a heat she had never before experienced. Burning through her was a new way of knowing and experiencing a man.

For a moment, a great stillness surrounded them, as though the moment were being captured and recorded for all time. The crowd held their breath as one, and in the back of the house, where he always sat, a cherubic smile brightened the features of Father Raymundo's face. With his right hand, he made the sign of the cross and said a prayer.

Estrella was the first to move. She stepped forward, advancing upon Sabicas; silently this time, upon the tips of her toes. She moved as though floating, gliding around his chair as he trilled a mysterious tremor in D minor, gathering energy from the dark sounds, building momentum.

The shell of Estrella's reserve cracked and she lowered her head, advancing toward Sabicas. Leaping out of his seat, he stepped aside as she made a series of adventurous passes, working her skirt, twisting and turning sharply into his sounds.

Inspired by the pure authority of her movements, he found within himself a new music. Long before the notes had reached him, they were already his; each sound a revelation, quickening new life into his veins, summoning sensation. Watching her move as he played, his heart pulsed with demand: *I want, I want, I want.* Already, he was addicted to Estrella, for she was in his blood.

"Work with me!" She cried out with abandon, her voice raspy and happy. She stepped lively around and about him, twisting and turning into the sharp shifts of his brisk tempo, pushed to the brink of form.

And just as a glass full of wine will spill when meeting robustly with another glass, so too did her happiness spill over the edges of her movements. Some in the crowd, unable to contain themselves, jumped out of their seats. Old ladies put their hands to their head, the younger ones to their heart.

"*Andelez, andelez!*" She teased out of his guitar all manner of sound, the likes of which he had never before produced. It was a fresh delivery; a brand new musicality was born through them, coming alive, changing them both.

She was a conjure woman, at one with his element. Raising the flame of his fire and rushing the flow of his blood, she stimulated. She was at play, working his mind, his talent and even his heart; drawing out all manner of strum.

The crowd felt it. Somehow the volatility of their passion had managed to heat every molecule of air in the room, penetrating all movement and sound; exploding inside the mind.

Playing for, and with, and through her, Sabicas delivered a new form. It was an immaculate conception. The best days of his life were about to begin, he knew.

A shrill scream of wonder pierced the air; someone in the audience had fainted from excitement. A man tore his shirt from off his back, and threw it on to the stage, where upon Estrella stamped at it with her foot, as though it were on fire. The performance was entering into a certain heat and pathos. Everyone's hair stood on end.

Used to bearing her soul, Estrella was not about to stop now before Sabicas; she knew well that he was the one for whom she had been waiting. Astonished by the turn of events, she turned to face him, whispering in her sweet raspy voice, "What took you so long?" And Sabicas replied with a courtly *rodeña*, as though serenading her from beneath her bedroom window: *I am here, and you are there, and we are here; together.*

Above La Café de la Alegrìa, the moon was particularly dazzling that night.

The Third Thing

After an hour on stage, Sabicas and Estrella knew each other well enough to know they wanted to know each other even better. Hand in hand, they left the stage amidst cheerful shouts and applause.

"What next?" They were his first words to her.

"We could take a walk to the Alameda or perhaps have a glass of wine," Estrella suggested.

He frowned. "I'd rather to do the third thing."

"The third thing?" She tilted her head.

"Get married," he said simply, as though the question of marriage was somehow preordained; the next logical step after such a rousing performance.

"It can be arranged." Estrella smiled wide, her gold tooth gleaming. She raised her hand above her head and snapped her fingers, and within seconds, Father Raymundo appeared, ready to conduct the wedding ceremony. Sabicas's eyebrows shot up in surprise.

Tzigany stepped forward with a few bands that he had removed from around his cigars. "Might you need rings?"

Sabicas smiled broadly at the charming cigar bands that Tzigany offered. "Thank you brother, but I have rings," he reached into his wallet and pulled out two golden wedding bands. "I keep them handy, just in case. One can never be too careful." He winked at Estrella.

Father Raymundo turned to Sabicas, "Sabicas, do you take Estrella to be your wife, to love her, to respect her, and to protect her, abandoning all others and dedicating yourself only to her?"

"I do!" Sabicas replied.

"And Estrella, do you take Sabicas to be your husband, to love him, to respect him, and to protect him, abandoning all others and dedicating yourself only to him?"

"I do!"

Rings were placed upon the other's finger and they kissed. A bucket of rice was brought out from the kitchen, and handfuls tossed over their heads.

Tzigany shot a finger up into the air. "A married couple must have their own Matrimonial Bed!"

"Do you have one to spare?" Sabicas asked.

"I do have one to spare and it is yours. Follow me!"

Estrella and Sabicas followed Tzigany across the street to the workshop while the café crowd reassembled itself into a wedding party. Spilling out of the cafe onto the street, they brought with them high spirits and an air of festivity. Cheerful laughter filled the night air and musicians played happy songs suited to the occasion. Surprising us all, La Chicarona lent her voice to a heartfelt *alboreas*. Considered a song of great purity, an *alboreas* is a song of Gypsy origin that is heard only at weddings and at no other time.

As La Chicarona sang, Father Raymundo handed out votive candles to one and all. Inside every heart, love, and above every candle, a smiling face.

Sabicas's head spun. Behold, thought he, a very strange

place is this wild little city of Ronda! The evening had begun
with the sound of a fine footstep breaking into his performance, and from out of the darkness, Estrella had appeared,
dancing before him in such a way as to change his world
forever. And then, no sooner had he proposed to her, but a
priest materialized out of thin air to conduct their wedding
ceremony! Now this: The great Tzigany was leading him in
the direction of a charmed Matrimonial Bed. The night was
unfolding like a myth all around! What next, he wondered,
pulling Estrella close.

La Paseo de la Camio de Matrimonio

With Alma and Elvira's help, I presented Estrella with
a selection of bed coverings and she quickly chose an Ara-
bic white and gold ensemble. It was richly textured velvet
damask with intricate Moroccan embroidery sewn into the
fabric. The drapery also featured embroidery and cascaded
like a delicate silken veil.

Tzigany opened wide the sliding doors of the workshop,
calling out to the revelers on the street, "I need ten strong
men to carry the bed to Estrella's apartment!"

At once, twenty men from the wedding party stepped
forward. Tzigany was relieved to see so many helpful hands,
for the bed was very heavy indeed. He pointed to the center of the bed, indicating to Estrella and Sabicas that they
were to climb aboard and prepare themselves for a wedding
procession. One does not ask questions of a fairy tale and

so the newlyweds did as they were told; positioning themselves in the center of the bed with their heads resting against the headboard, delighted by the spontaneous magic of the moment that Tzigany had created on their behalf. Sabicas squeezed her hand and plump joyful tear drops rolled down Estrella's cheek.

The men took up their stations around the bed, honored to play such a helpful role. On the count of three, they raised the bed upon their shoulders and walked it out of the workshop in slow measured steps. Tzigany led the way, calling out every bump of the old and winding road, warning of curbs and dips, lest anyone lose their footing.

When at last Estrella closed her eyes and threw her wedding bouquet out into the crowd, it was Elvira's old and wrinkled hands that caught it. Senor Perez caught her eye and between them there passed a meaningful look.

A window shutter banged open above the crowd, and a sleepy little boy poked his head into the night air, "What's going on down there?" he shouted out, rubbing his eyes.

"Estrella de la Flamenca just got married!"

His eyes widened. "Mama, papa! Estrella de la Flamenca got married!"

The parents appeared at the window.

"Congratulations Estrella! Wait! Who is her husband? Let's go down and see!"

All the way down the road, wooden shutters banged open, heads popping out into the night air, and one by one, they all descended upon the street, joining the celebration.

"The more the merrier!" Father Raymundo said, handing out votive candles to the newcomers. Somebody had apparently made a telephone call to the local newspaper, for a smiling photographer arrived on the scene upon a moped, tooting a ridiculous sounding horn with glee. He parked on the sidewalk, jumped off the moped and quickly flashed a few photographs of the newlyweds for the paper, before bearing some of the weight of the bed upon his own shoulders.

Upon the bed, the love birds nestled in one another's arms. Held aloft by their friends and fans, the evening's performance symbolized the beginning of a lifetime of love.

When we arrived at Estrella's apartment, the Matrimonial Bed had to be dismantled, carried up a flight of stairs, and reassembled inside of her bedroom, but with so many helping hands, the task was easily handled, leaving Elvira Vega, Alma and I to dress the bed once again in its finery.

Alma sang a *cante chico*; a lighthearted little folk song, and we all joined in as we plumped up the pillows, and smoothed out the wrinkles of the sheets. Elvira struck a match, lighting the tapered beeswax candles of the candelabra upon Estrella's dresser.

In the soft glow of candlelight, the bed's enchantments were magnified, and linking arms, we stood before it in admiration. Elvira's eyes were dazzled by what she saw and she whistled long and low. "What great Mystery school did Tzigany attend?"

Her canny assessment of Tzigany's formal training was right on the mark; there is much to learn and none of it from a book. Tzigany had deepened the knowledge of his craft from a master who used unconventional methods to prime the subconscious mind; a prerequisite if one wishes to hasten the rise to one's greatness. Exploring the inner space of his creativity, Tzigany learned things that were not taught anywhere else in the world. His instructor was descended from a long line of well connected teachers, all of whom had helped to inspire some of the most artistically alive creators in all of Spain: Picasso, Lorca, Carmen Amaya, and it was hinted Ferran Adria, to name but a few. Artists were blindfolded in order to become better painters and poets were denied the use of words with which to express themselves. As a carpenter of luxurious Matrimonial Beds, Tzigany was instructed to sleep upon a bed of nails. A bizarre training ground to be sure, but highly effective in concentrating ones vision. There is more to being a bed maker than just making beds, as Tzigany likes to say, whilst tapping at the temple of his imagination.

Elvira sighed. "I am going to have to get one of these beds for myself!"

"Tzigany sells only to newlyweds." Alma teased.

"Then I will get married!" Elvira shot back.

While Elvira and Alma exchanged laughing remarks, I felt myself go quiet inside, imagining the beauty of Estrella and Sabicas in the bed, doing what happy couples do.

"Enough," I said, "We had better go now, and let the newlyweds be."

The three of us descended upon the street. The wedding party had long since departed and so all was quiet.

Standing just outside the threshold to the building, Father Raymundo bestowed blessings upon the newlyweds, and we heard snippets of sound wisdom as we passed them by.

"Marriages are not about show, costumes or glamour," he told them, "but the simple things that happen behind the scenes." He spoke softly, with a gentle sweetness that charmed the air all around.

Tzigany, Juan and Senor Perez stood beneath the light of a street lamp on the street corner, all of them puffing upon cigars.

Handsome old Senor Perez leaned upon his cane. A haze of smoke surrounded him, lending him a mysterious air. He tipped his hat at Elvira. "Are you ready for that drink?"

"I am indeed." She replied.

We were all riding upon a fine wave of joy, the momentum of which had us moving idly towards La Café de la Alegrìa to share one last bottle of wine.

❦ ❦

End of Book One

The Gypsy Chronicles continues...

Look for Book Two:
Charmed and Dangerous
at a bookstore near you — soon!

www.TheGypsyChronicles.com
www.AlisonMackie.com

A Note to Readers

from Alison Mackie

The Gypsy Chronicles is a fantastic choice for your Book Reading Group!

I will chat by speakerphone with any book reading group that has read *The Gypsy Chronicles*, to discuss its message more deeply.

To schedule a free conference call, please send your request to Ashton Court Press at www.TheGypsyChronicles.com.

Simply complete the request form located on the contact page. Please note that all requests must be converted to EST, between 11 A.M. and 9 P.M.

Your request will be honored within days.

www.TheGypsyChronicles.com

Acknowledgments

Kathleen Edwards
of the Naples Media Group, Inc.

Like a fairy godmother with a magical wand, you waved your design savvy over *The Gypsy Chronicles*, enchanting it with visual charm. Because of you, the book is a gem; a treasure to both hold, and to behold. Your vision is pure authority. I thank you.

Coleman Barks

Thank you for allowing me use of your poems: Like a favorite pair of slippers, they were a cozy fit with my own words and ideas. Their ancient wisdom added layers of meaning.

Ernest Hole of www.ImageSpain.com

Your archive of old fashioned postcards, illustrations and photographs is a Spanish national treasure. Thank you for your generosity in allowing me use of your rare and utterly delightful images.

Meredith Blevins

Wise woman of the word. Thank you so much for reading my manuscript at a most critical stage in its development. Without your astute comments, *The Gypsy Chronicles* would not have evolved in the way that it did.

John Mackie

Instead of reading my manuscript at a most critical stage in its development you opted to wait for the movie, instead. This is a good thing, and I thank you, for if you had commented upon *The Gypsy Chronicles*, it would have evolved into a Scottish detective novel.

Angicaro

Thank you for being who you are in the world, for your beautiful name, and for your soul-baring self portraits on Flickr.com.

George Borrow

Your accounts of the Gypsies in Spain served as an inspiration.

Fredrico Garcia Lorca

Your essay, *The Theory and Play of the Duende*, fed my imagination, informed my words, and inspired many scenes within the story. Many thanks.

In Spain, I give credit to the Spanish wine maker whose powerful gaze hastened my movements toward writing *The Gypsy Chronicles*:

Several years ago, while flipping through *Food and Wine* magazine, I came across the photo of a Spanish wine maker. His eyes glowed with a power that is difficult to describe. If I told you he had the gaze of a bull fighter you would know well what I mean. Steady, intense and bold. But there was something other ... something I could not wrap my head around, and so I carried his photograph with me for days, trying to figure out what that something was. Finally, I hit upon it. His gaze was full of duende; a powerful force of creativity. I looked into his eyes and saw that he was a man of his world, that he was living his dream in creating his fine wines. Understanding this, I questioned my own life. It had been years since I was creatively engaged. I had been wandering around half alive, and his eyes brought me back to life. At that moment, *The Gypsy Chronicles* was born. I placed the photo of the Spanish wine maker above my desk and began to write a tale. I had only to gaze at his image and a new character or twist in the plot would make itself known; such was the power of my muse.

I am grateful to A.S. Kline for allowing me to base my condensed versions of Lorca upon his translations. For Saint Teresa of Avila, Cher, Mae West and Anais Nin, I am very grateful.

In the USA, I am thankful for Brother-Johnny, Tom Williams, Denise Hinds, Nancy Pinter, Wanda Stanfill, Anne Neuman and especially New Zealand Kim - my loverly pool lady, who allowed me to read long passages aloud to her from the book as she worked.

And in the United Kingdom: Thank you Anne Hamilton and John Speirs of Ensinger Ltd., my very first readers and enthusiastic supporters.

In India, I thank my mother who taught me that True Love is better than a bar of chocolate. In Heaven, my father the gambler, who taught me how to take bold risks, apparently. In Canada, I thank the good woman of Salt Spring Island: Sandy Buyze-Morgan. In France, I am grateful for Just Jaekin's sweet film, *Le Dernier Amant Romantique*. In Spain, special thanks to Paco Sanchez, Spanish Flamenco photographer, of Expofoto. com. And to my E-muses who reside all over the map, outer space included: Our correspondences served as a powerful training ground. Through you I learned not only how to use words to capture attention, but more importantly, how to keep that attention. *Muchos Gracias!*

About the Author

Alison Mackie

Although born in Seville, I was conceived in Alsace-Lorraine, France, a region well known for its wine. And so it passed that my parents named me Alison Lorraine, sure that I would one day become a connoisseur of fine wines. As a child, I was expected to know good wine from bad. For me, it was easy: If the wine hurt my teeth, it was bad. I faked it most of the time, but my parents encouraged me, and later in life I became a wine promoter. First and foremost however, I'm a family woman.

What qualifies me to write about Gypsies?

During my formative years in Seville, I had an Andalusian Gypsy nanny by the name of Ahalita. Unable to bear children of her own, Ahalita poured all of her maternal affection upon me. She was a flamenco dancer and no sooner was my mother gone for her day's outing, than Ahalita would place a flamenco record upon the turn table. I remember waking up from my afternoon naps to see Ahalita hovering over my crib, holding my chubby little wrist and twisting my hand around and around, training me towards the flamenco. To this day, I still twirl my wrists upon awakening.

From her own coin, Ahalita fitted me out in flamenco dresses and extravagant bracelets. On our morning walks through the park, she presented me to all as though I was her own. My mother felt her intense feelings for me bordered upon obsession, and as Ahalita's connection with me deepened, so too did my mother's sense of unease. The time had come to let her go. Ahalita did not take kindly to being fired, but that is a story for another time.

I feel that the residue of Ahalita's spirit is somehow linked with my own. I may not have Gypsy blood flowing through my veins, but I have something of Ahalita, that is a certainty. There is an old Spanish saying: *More grows in the garden than the planter has sown.*

Alison studied creative writing at Kwantlen, in British Columbia with Jane Munro and Chris Rideout. She lives in Southwest Florida.

Photo by Denise Morris